---- ★ ----

"We didn't know her. For as bad a shape as she was in, she'd been tidied up a bit before they tucked her in that basket. Who would bother to do that, if you don't know her and care about her? Poor thing, lying there, curled up like a puppy, but all funny colored and unsettled looking. She must have fought back. Poor thing had a horrible bruise on her cheek, and only one earring on."

"What wounds did she have? Tidied up how?" he asked intently.

Suspicion dawned on the housekeeper's face. "Who did you say you were?"

J.J. tried to find something innocent but compelling to say that would make him sound official without actually sounding like he was representing himself that way. It took too long.

The woman stood up. "I'm no fool. You told me not to talk with those women so I'd talk to you." Her lined face registered fear. "How do I know you aren't the one who killed her?"

---- ★ ----

Previously published Worldwide Mystery title by
JULIE WRAY HERMAN

THREE DIRTY WOMEN AND THE GARDEN OF DEATH

JULIE WRAY HERMAN

THREE DIRTY WOMEN AND THE BITTER BREW

WORLDWIDE®

TORONTO • NEW YORK • LONDON
AMSTERDAM • PARIS • SYDNEY • HAMBURG
STOCKHOLM • ATHENS • TOKYO • MILAN
MADRID • WARSAW • BUDAPEST • AUCKLAND

To my children, Edward and Anne, and to my husband,
Paul. Thank you for the support you've given me.
May you always have dreams toward which you reach—
and people you love with whom to travel along the
way—it makes the journey worthwhile.

THREE DIRTY WOMEN AND THE BITTER BREW

A Worldwide Mystery/January 2006

First published by Silver Dagger Mysteries.

ISBN 0-373-26552-2

Printed in U.S.A.

Acknowledgments

Thank you to everyone who lent a kind ear, or who gave me information I needed to finish this book. It's been a great year, and I've met so many wonderful people who love books and the worlds they open up for us. My apologies to everyone I misled about the tea thing—trust me, it's better this way.

To Mr. Bucky Burnsed of the Savannah Police Department: Thank you for patiently answering my questions about your department; any mistakes I have made are surely not your fault.

To our Savannah cousin, Bobby Herman, for pointing me in the right direction to have those questions answered.

To Megan and Dean: Your honesty is so precious.

To my Buds, who kept me laughing.

To Stacey, for the cover. You can design my garden anytime!

And to all the folks at Overmountain: Thank you so much for making this possible.

CAST OF CHARACTERS

Bascom, J. J.: Pine Grove Chief of Police;
Janey Bascom's husband

Bascom, Janey: partner in Three Dirty Women
Landscaping; married to J. J. Bascom

Colthurst, Richard: attorney; Chaz McFaile's friend
from Law School; resident of Savannah

Gilcrest, Leo: president of the Small Landscapers
League

Halloran, Dodie: Korine McFaile's roommate at the
Small Landscapers Conference in Savannah

McFaile, Chaz: Korine McFaile's son; attorney;
recently relocated to Savannah

McFaile, Korine: senior partner in Three Dirty Women
Landscaping; mother of Chaz McFaile; widow of
Charlie McFaile

Sudley: detective from the Savannah Police
Department; in charge of the case at hand

Whittier, Amilou: partner in Three Dirty Women
Landscaping; unable to attend conference due to events
in GARDEN OF DEATH

Winslow, George: husband of Sharon Winslow

Winslow, Holly: college co-ed daughter of Sharon and
George Winslow

Winslow, Sharon: wife of George Winslow; cousin
of Dodie Halloran; organizer of the twelfth annual
Southern Small Landscapers Conference

ONE

"YOU HANDCUFFED THE WOMAN on your first date?" Korine McFaile exclaimed.

J.J. Bascom replied, "It was the only way I could go home in one piece. I happened to have brought them along. Want to borrow them?"

"I don't think Dodie Halloran would sit still long enough for me to put handcuffs on her like your date did. Dodie hates me. I just wish I knew why," Korine said.

The two sat skulking behind the potted palms in the lobby of the Savannah Hilliard Hotel. Korine and Janey Bascom, two-thirds of the partnership of Three Dirty Women Landscaping, Inc., were attending the twelfth annual Southern Small Landscapers Conference. So far, barely an hour into the opening cocktail party, Korine had almost forgotten that she prided herself on being a tolerant person.

Janey came around the corner with a plate of food for J.J. The slim woman slid in behind the swaying fronds and sat next to her husband on the overstuffed couch. He put an arm around his wife and tucked her in next to him. Janey's smooth café-au-lait coloring and J.J.'s weathered good looks made them a striking couple. Opposites only in their looks, the two of them comple-mented each other's lives in all the ways that counted.

Originally, Janey and Korine were going to room to-gether. Then J.J. had the bright idea to come along and keep Janey company. After the grueling hour Korine had spent in her room with Dodie, she almost wished he'd stayed home to take care of business as Pine Grove's chief of police.

Their third partner, Amilou Whittier, had not been able to convince her probation officer that going to Sa-vannah, Georgia, didn't violate the terms of her sen-tence. The previous summer, following the murder of Amilou's husband, Judge Carrolton had saddled her with what some critics were calling a very light sentence for her crimes. To hear Amilou, the sentence was en-tirely too strict, given the extenuating circumstances. Korine privately agreed with those who criticized the judge in the case. Amilou still didn't seem to realize the magnitude of what she had done.

"If I didn't think it would take measures that would cost me my job," J.J. kidded, "I'd offer to convince Dodie that she shouldn't bother you anymore."

"That's not necessary." Korine smiled in spite of her-self at the vision of Dodie handcuffed to a chair some-where, leaving her free to attend the conference in peace. "If all else fails, I'll just move in with you two."

The silent exchange of panicked looks between her two friends made Korine laugh outright. "Never mind, I'll make it through the weekend in one piece. I just wish I'd taken the trouble to find my own roommate, instead of relying on Sharon. She's got more than enough on her plate organizing all this without having to run a roommate matching service at the same time."

She regarded J.J. and Janey with something approaching her usual humor. Thank goodness she had friends like the two of them. Even though J.J. had inadvertently caused the problem, the pair of them were also the saving grace of the weekend. Korine's son, Chaz, had moved to Savannah not too long before, and he promised to be a much-needed distraction when he picked her up the next day for a sight-seeing tour of the city. Still, she knew that she'd have gone absolutely insane if Janey and J.J. weren't there to help her regain a proper perspective on things.

From the minute Korine had walked into her room, Dodie started complaining about anything and everything—almost as if she was trying deliberately to ruin Korine's weekend. Korine hadn't even been able to unpack her clothes without being treated to the woman's helpful criticisms.

Janey held up the conference program and asked, "Have you decided what sessions you're interested in yet?"

"There's one on soils," Korine said, plunging her hand deep within the blue canvas tote bag she'd received when they checked in. She first pulled out a handful of advertisements, making enough room for her questing fingers to find the slick surface of the program. She opened it and thumbed through. "They've got Steve Bender from *Southern Living* doing 'Dishing up Good Dirt.' Soil is the underpinning of all good gardens."

When J.J. groaned, Korine gave him a quick grin of appreciation for his having caught her drift. "I love his column so much, I can't miss that." She turned the page. "There's another one first thing in the morning, Bill Welch on antique roses."

A flushed round face sporting bifocals peered through the fronds like a disembodied owl. "Korine?" the vision breathlessly inquired. "You in there?"

"Sharon." Korine stood up and shoved the pot over so that the heavyset woman could get by. "We're just deciding which part of the conference to attend first."

"I thought that was you mentioning the roses," Sharon said. "Bill Welch sure knows his stuff." The woman's coiffed hair didn't stir an inch as she nodded vigorously. She was the same age as Korine but looked and acted ten years older. "I'm a little worried about that seminar on composting. I'm not so sure anyone will be there at all. I mean," she said, her tone conveying disdain in every syllable, "how much is there to throwing all your rotting stuff in a heap and waiting it out?"

Janey ducked her head behind her program. There was a man not far outside Pine Grove who pulled in a very nice salary from recycled horse manure. Korine avoided looking in Janey's direction as she answered noncommittally. Composting had come a long way from burying kitchen scraps out in the back corner of the yard.

"Now, before I forget," Sharon said, "Dodie mentioned a little tiff between the two of you?"

Korine shifted uncomfortably in her seat. What was

Dodie thinking of, pulling Sharon into their squabble? Korine felt a stab of anger. Despite her personal distaste, she had bent over backwards to be polite. "We'll work it out on our own," she said neutrally.

"I would have thought so too, but the poor thing was in tears. I wouldn't have thought it of you."

"Sharon," J.J. said, "that woman could sell you the hind end off a donkey and make you think you'd gotten the better half."

Janey's gentle touch on J.J.'s arm got his attention and he bit off whatever he had been about to add.

Sharon blinked from J.J.'s set face to Korine's inflamed one. "I see," she said, and Korine could see the wheels turning. "I thought y'all would enjoy getting to know each other better since Dodie's moved up to your part of the country. I may have made an error in judgment."

"I don't actually know Dodie, but her reputation goes before her. I should have said something to you before we got into the room." Korine paused, and out of the corner of her eye she caught an odd look on Janey's face. Sharon's obvious misery aroused Korine's sense of pity. She repeated her pledge: "You've got plenty to worry with over the conference, Sharon. Dodie and I will work out our differences on our own."

"I hope so. I don't think I can stand any more personality conflicts." Sharon flipped the fern back behind her head and cruised out into the crowd.

"How did I wind up being the villain?" Korine demanded.

Janey said, "I overheard them talking at registration.

Dodie and Sharon are cousins. I should have said something much sooner."

"Oh my." Korine was aghast. Neither Sharon nor Dodie had so much as breathed a word of this earlier.

J.J. broke the silence. "I don't know about the two of you, but I want some more of that food before it's all gone. You can't let Dodie keep you hostage just because she's unpleasant."

"You're right, of course. And you'll be there with your handcuffs if she gets out of hand." Korine stood up, smoothed her skirt, and tucked a stray piece of fluffy gray hair behind her ears.

J.J.'s neck flushed as he looked sternly at Korine.

"Sorry," she said at the same time that Janey said, "What do you mean?"

"Long story, honey," J.J. said, slipping an arm around Janey. He gave Korine a mock hard stare. "Let's go see what's left, and I'll tell you all about it."

"WHAT DO YOU MEAN talking about me behind my back?" Dodie's tearful voice came from behind Korine as she reached for a veggie cornucopia.

Korine deposited the canapé on her plate and slowly turned to face the woman. "Dodie, Sharon said that you had complained about me. I told her that we'd settle whatever differences we had. In *private?*"

The stress on the last word went right by Dodie. Looking like a stuffed pimento in her tight red sheath, Dodie's face was blotched and tearstained. "It's a bit late to keep this private, don't you think?"

Thanks to her shrill voice, Dodie was absolutely correct. Heads were turning in an ever-widening circle. Soon the entire ballroom would be witness to this hissy fit.

"Dodie, for goodness' sake, I don't want to be at odds with you. After all, we have to live with each other for the rest of this weekend. How about we go sit down and see if we can find out what's going on here."

"You publicly malign my reputation? And when I call you on it, you want to go somewhere and sit down and chat?" Dodie's voice carried clearly beyond the buffet table to those shamelessly listening from their seats.

"I have no idea what you're talking about." Korine was beginning to feel as if she'd stepped in quicksand. This woman's problems were far more serious than she'd earlier thought.

"I was willing to give you some benefit of the doubt when Sharon told me who I would be rooming with. For all I knew, you weren't the white trash who named the company Three Dirty Women." Dodie delivered this into dead silence. Every ear in the place was tuned in to see what the latest scandal was about.

Korine opened her mouth to reply. She was saved from what indignation might have inspired her to say by a smooth, deep voice coming from behind her.

"Ladies, if you'll allow me to help, we may be able to sort this out." Leo Gilcrest, the current president of the Small Landscapers League, cut the two of them out of line and steered them both firmly to his table.

While not exactly private, it did afford Korine the opportunity to lower herself into a chair. As soon as she sat down, she realized how badly her legs were shaking.

As Dodie opened her mouth, Leo held up one hand to stop her. "I know that you've had your feelings hurt, Dodie," he said. "But Korine doesn't usually speak poorly of folks. Maybe Sharon misunderstood."

Korine wondered with whom he had been speaking. She didn't remember having met him before. She'd read his articles in the newsletter, and she thought he knew his plants pretty well. She'd heard rumors about him, though. If the stories told about him were true, he knew his way around the ladies even better than he knew his botany.

Dodie pressed her lips together, accentuating the lines that ran from her pinched nose down to her chin. Throwing Korine a look that could kill, she crossed her arms over her chest and exhaled deeply.

"Now as I understand it, you two were assigned to room together and haven't hit it off?" Leo's voice was hypnotic, low and rumbly, causing Korine's mind to wander.

She firmly yanked it back. Her husband had been dead seven years, but this was the first time she'd taken notice of a man since she'd lost Charlie. Poor timing and, given those notorious stories, a poor choice on her part. She had no misgivings about ruthlessly suppressing the lingering attraction she felt. A nagging feeling of familiarity tugged at her, caused, no doubt, by all the rumors that trailed Leo in his wake.

Dodie didn't seem to have that trouble. Leaning forward, her expression softened until she looked for all the world like a lost kitten who'd found the Holy Grail, filled to the rim with cream. She reached out and batted his arm. "Leo, you know how I get when people say mean things."

"Yes, but I wish you'd find out if people really did say those things before attacking them." He took her hand and squeezed it. The smoldering look that passed between them told Korine that her instinct to steer clear of this man had been correct. His conquest sat before him, one who would scratch Korine's eyes out in a heartbeat.

"I don't know what Sharon told you," Korine began. She tried to smile at Dodie, but indignation had robbed her of that ability. "It's true that you and I didn't exactly hit it off. But I don't know you well enough to have said anything really horrible about you."

Dodie's eyes narrowed as she considered Korine. "I guess I should apologize for flying off the handle. It happens sometimes."

"I'm more than happy to apologize also, but I wish I knew what I was supposed to be apologizing for before I start."

Leo sat back, the telltale creak of the folding chair betraying his size. "Dodie, what did Sharon tell you?"

Dodie turned to Korine. "If you were that unhappy with me as your roommate, I wish you'd told me instead of going to Sharon with those accusations. I know I'm new to this landscaping thing, but I'm trying as hard as I can to learn."

Korine stared at her. She hadn't said word one about Dodie's gardening skill, or lack thereof, mostly because she didn't know anything at all about it. She opened her mouth and said so.

"But Sharon said—"

"Cross my heart," Korine interrupted. "I did not say any such thing." Looking steadily into Dodie's eyes, she saw something human flicker in the hazel depths, then die down.

"Well then. I guess y'all are friends again." Leo sounded as pleased with himself as could be. "Let me go get a plate for you two ladies, then we can sit down together and visit some about more pleasant things."

When neither of them objected, he returned to the buffet and armed himself with two more plates. Watching him balance them on one arm as he piled on enough food for an army, Korine shook off the feeling of familiarity that Leo Gilcrest inspired in her. How had he gotten under her skin so quickly?

She turned to Dodie and said, "Maybe we should start all over again." She put her hand out to shake.

Dodie stared at it. Again that strange flicker aroused itself in the back of Dodie's eyes, making her seem almost vulnerable. It was fleeting, and her face regained its predatory mask, like a lioness on the hunt. She reached out and took Korine's hand gingerly between three fingers, a genteel Southern lady's handshake. "Friends," Dodie said.

"Friends," Korine repeated as Leo put the overfull plates in front of them. She spent the rest of the meal wondering how Dodie planned to get back at her. That Dodie planned to be friendly anywhere except in Leo's company never entered her mind.

TWO

KORINE WAS UP and in the shower early the next morning. Her head already hurt. Dodie, as it turned out, was not just a harridan during the day. She snored.

Rinsing the last of the shampoo out of her hair, Korine allowed herself a blissful moment. The hammer of the hot water against the wisps of gray hair on the back of her neck eased the cramping pain. Little by little, Korine felt her body relax. Her emotions followed suit. The humor of the predicament occurred to her, and she started to laugh. Silently, of course. Dodie had made it very clear the night before that she required her beauty sleep.

As Korine stepped out of the shower, she realized that her caution had been unnecessary. Through the thin particleboard door, she heard Dodie talking to someone.

Dodie's angry tone came through loud and clear, although Korine had to make up the words to go with it. She heard an answering murmur. There wasn't enough force behind the second voice to tell if the person was trying to placate Dodie or tell her to jump out the window. Apparently, beauty sleep wasn't enough to make up for the woman's personality.

Korine's head began to throb again. There was an

echoing pounding on the bathroom door. She gave the door the evil eye.

"Hold on to your britches!" she muttered under her breath. Quickly she toweled off, dragged her bathrobe on, then threw open the still-quivering door.

"And don't come crawling back anytime soon!" Dodie shouted. She whirled around. "What are you staring at?" she demanded of Korine.

The door to the hallway was just closing behind the person with whom Dodie had been arguing.

"Who was that?"

"Your friends have an indecent idea of what time to come knocking on doors," Dodie said. Her hair had lost its lacquered shell while she'd slept, making her look more human than Korine had seen to date. As Dodie noticed Korine taking in the state of her hair, she put a hand up to smooth what could only be a cowlick back down into her bangs.

Korine had been afraid that the pulled-together look Dodie had sported the day before was tattooed on rather than achieved. For a moment, a small moment, Korine felt like smiling at her roommate.

Dodie swept past Korine into the bathroom, shutting the door firmly behind her. Korine heard the snick of the lock as Dodie shot it home. The sound of running water gave testament to the fact that Dodie wasn't coming out again and that Korine was now on the opposite side of the door from her clothes.

She did not understand the woman. Korine could have sworn that she had seen an answering smile in

Dodie's eyes before she fled into the bathroom. *How pitiful it must be to be afraid to make friends,* Korine thought. *And how lonely.*

Knowing that the skirt and blouse she had hung up on the back of the bathroom door might not survive Dodie's morning ritual, she turned to the closet and selected another outfit.

FIFTEEN MINUTES LATER, Korine knocked gently on Janey and J.J.'s door. "That woman is so sad," she announced as Janey let her in.

"That bad?"

"Dodie Halloran makes it harder to figure out her reason for being than tending impatiens in August. I think there might be a human being in there somewhere under the hair spray and tight clothes, but she goes to such lengths to hide that fact, it's not worth the effort to find out." Korine dropped into the chair Janey offered and propped her elbows on the table in front of her, the better to support her aching head in her hands.

She continued, "I just spent ten minutes talking to the desk clerk, Javier, checking, just in case I needed to get a room of my own. It can't be done. This hotel is full to the gills with gardeners."

Janey sat down in the other chair and slid a warm brown mug filled with hot black coffee across the table. Korine picked it up gratefully. Taking a large swallow, she felt the liquid burn its way down her throat. Sucking in a quick breath, she blew across the top of the clunky mug.

Janey cradled a mug of her own in her hands, regarding the swirl of steam coming off its surface for a moment. Tightening her grip on the handle, Janey lifted it to her lips for a sip. "Does it help to think of her sitting there handcuffed to the bar while her date walks out on her?" she asked, deadpan.

Korine laughed. Dodie's antics retreated into the proper perspective.

Janey snuggled back into her chair. "Now that I've pictured Dodie handcuffed, I don't know if I can keep a straight face when I see her again."

"I should have kept that incident in mind last night. Did you hear her?"

"Who didn't?" Janey responded. She shrugged. "Anyone who knows you won't give it a second thought."

"And everyone who doesn't will avoid me like the plague today."

"Drink your coffee," Janey commanded. "And quit feeling sorry for yourself."

Korine smiled back at her friend. "Where is J.J.?"

"He went out to find some breakfast."

Impulsively, Korine leaned across the table and squeezed Janey's hand. "I am so glad that you and J.J. found each other."

"Not half as glad as I am. When I first met him, I thought he was so much like Raynell that I could never be in the same room with him without panicking. I'd made such a mistake with that first marriage I was afraid to even go out with anyone, much less another Southern White Male."

"You couldn't have found anyone less like Raynell," Korine agreed. "I know I've told you this before, but it still pleases me no end that you left him and that you found the courage to try again with J.J. Sometimes I think you're invincible."

Janey's gaze shifted away from Korine's. "Not in the ways that count." Unconsciously, Janey's hand went down to cradle her stomach.

She had suffered a miscarriage a few months earlier. If Korine could have handed her friend a healed heart, she would have done so in an instant. Janey had weathered the loss of the baby surprisingly well. The episode had tempered her, rather than having caused a return of her panic attacks, Raynell's hellish legacy. Still, these small unconscious gestures told Korine how much Janey still mourned the loss of their child.

Janey removed her hand and picked up her coffee. "It took me a long time to even think about dating. Thank goodness J.J. had the sense to wait until I'd gotten my feet back under me before ever asking me out. I might have run fast and hard back to Louisiana if he'd asked me out even one day sooner than he did."

"Has he told you how hard it was to wait that long?" Korine asked.

Janey nodded, a shy smile unfolding across her face.

"I'll never forget the look on his face when we walked in the door at the police station that first time," Korine said. "Your face was all a mess, split lip, bruised, and everything. I thought he was going to kill Raynell."

"He told me as much on our first date. J.J. had a sister who didn't leave her husband in time."

"I didn't know that," Korine said. "She died?"

"One of the reasons J.J. went into law enforcement in the first place," Janey replied. She took another long sip of her coffee before looking shyly up at Korine. "We're trying again."

Korine's stomach tightened. She was surprised by the depth of her own reaction to Janey's loss. Even while Korine murmured soothing phrases, she relived the deep, lonely despair she thought she'd buried long ago. She'd always wanted more children, but it was not to be.

Firmly, she reminded herself that she had Dennis, the nephew she'd all but adopted, and his wife, Katie Ann, in addition to her own son, Chaz. Even if Chaz and Dennis didn't get along all that well, she still had a wonderful, full family tree. Nephews of her husband, Charlie, and her own sister's children filled the house to overflowing at holiday celebrations. Nothing to complain about.

Looking at her watch, Korine stood hurriedly. "We'd better get going before we miss the rosarian's lecture. Chaz is picking me up soon after that, so I don't want to miss the only thing I was going to do today at this conference."

Korine's son had recently joined his friend Richard in the Chatham County District Attorney's office. Private practice alone in Pine Grove hadn't suited his needs. Since he'd been less than communicative after the move, Korine was worried that their relationship might suffer from the distance.

Janey also rose. "I'll meet you there. I suppose I need to find J.J. He's probably still down at the breakfast buffet."

They both picked up their canvas bags. Janey slipped her key in her pocket, and the two women went out to catch the elevator.

THE ROOM ALLOCATED for featured speakers was much too small for the number of people at the conference. Korine squeezed in at the last minute, right before the door monitors barricaded the room. The fire marshal would have been appalled.

Bill Welch primed the audience well, proving beyond a shadow of a doubt that getting advice from experts could really enhance a landscaper's knowledge. After that, he turned off the lights to start his slide show.

As he pointed to a beautiful old rose specimen on the screen, Korine could see his lips move in profile. What she heard was a low, female voice hissing, "I don't think you understand."

Unable to identify who was speaking, or where the voice was coming from, several people shushed their neighbors.

"This one's a beauty," the speaker's lips said, lovingly tracing the contours of a Cherokee rose specimen that he'd placed along a split-rail fence.

Audible was a disembodied throaty whisper. "You back off, or I'll be forced to—"

There was a rustle, a shriek, and the lights came on.

Everyone looked at everyone else. Korine, at least,

knew for whom she was looking. Her erstwhile room-mate was nowhere to be seen. As the audience began to twitter, there was a loud thud, followed by more rustling. It came from the speakers, although the rosarian never moved. People looked at one another, restless in their seats. Snippets of conversation that Korine overheard around her ranged from amused to outraged.

Not a few of the audience looked at her, their attention sliding away like bald sneakers on ice when they saw her looking back. She wasn't the only one who had recognized Dodie's voice. After a moment, when all remained quiet, the rosarian dimmed the lights and continued his talk. Unable to concentrate, Korine took a step backward and pushed through the doorway behind her.

Janey was standing in the empty hallway, flipping pages in the conference program.

"I thought you were in there." Korine indicated the room behind her.

"I still haven't found J.J. Finally just gave up and came on down. Am I too late?"

"Something weird is going on with Dodie. I'm a little worried." Briefly, Korine described what she'd heard earlier through the bathroom door and over the PA in the room behind her.

"Where do you think it came from?"

Korine looked around and saw a sign announcing that the room next door to the one she had come out of would be the site of the next panel discussion of perennials. When consulted, Janey's program informed them that there would be a speaker in both rooms the rest of the day.

"I guess we could check and make sure everything's all right?" Korine asked. Remembering the way Dodie had treated her, Korine wasn't sure that she wanted to follow up on her intuition.

"Your imagination is running away with you," Janey replied. "You don't hurt people just because they irritate you to death."

Korine nodded, but her feet disagreed with her, marching her over to the door of the supposedly empty room. Janey sighed audibly but followed suit. Together they pushed open the door. Poking their heads though, they looked around. The room was empty. Dust motes danced overhead in the glare of the crystal chandelier. As Korine walked up to the dais, she caught the tail end of a lingering note of Chanel in the air, a mute testimony to the fact that the room had been inhabited shortly before.

Climbing up onto the platform, they circled the blue-skirted table loaded with recording equipment. Korine looked carefully and did indeed find a microphone with its switch in the "on" position. She reached over and flipped it off.

"Who was Dodie arguing with this time?" Janey asked.

"I have no idea. I think it was a man, but that's as much as I can say with any authority. It could have been the same person that she was yelling at this morning. Or it could be somebody completely different. Makes you wonder what her record is for the number of people she can antagonize in one day."

Janey shook with laughter. "If you could hear your

voice." With a sideways look from under her lashes at Korine, she continued, "With luck, it was Leo Gilcrest."

"Oh no," Korine demurred. "She wouldn't fight with him. He's got her wound around his little finger."

"But you'd like to have him wound around yours, wouldn't you?"

Korine gave Janey a sharp look. How did she know? "He's interested in Dodie."

"Dodie, my foot. You have more appeal than she does." Janey paused halfway to the door and turned to look seriously at Korine. "You've been missing Charlie for a long time." She hesitated, then shyly continued, "Leo does have nice shoulders—"

"Why thank you." Leo's deep voice sounded behind the women.

Korine jumped out of her skin, then exchanged a guilty look with a furiously blushing Janey. They swiveled around to find Leo Gilcrest, shoulders and all, standing on the dais.

"Where on earth did you come from?" Korine said, surprise making her snappy.

Indicating the service doors behind him, he said, "I moderate the first panel in here in an hour. I thought it prudent to come in and make sure that the room was ready." He indicated the jumble of wires and boxes in front of him and shrugged eloquently. Korine's sense of déjà vu deepened.

Leo leaned over, flipped the switch on the mike, and tapped it. When no noise came out, he frowned. "It must be broken," he said.

"I think it's connected to the speakers in the next room," Korine replied. She walked back to the dais and reached over to turn the microphone back off again.

"What?"

"I was in the room next door. Evidently the two systems are linked and—" Korine stopped and exchanged an uneasy glance with Janey. She decided not to tell him that Dodie had been arguing with someone in here just a few minutes earlier. Dodie might be a tattletale, but Korine most certainly was not.

"I wish that these technical people could get it straight which room we were taping and which room is not in use. Now we won't have anything to sell those folks who couldn't make it this morning." Leo's tone was angry. "This hotel staff is terrible. They've even put out dirty linens." He leaned over and brushed at a stain on the drape hanging around the table.

His hand came away smeared crimson. Korine froze for a second, staring at his palm.

The skin at Leo's neck had turned an awful shade of red, reminding Korine of Dodie's dress the night before, and he said, "Some idiot spilled a Bloody Mary in here and didn't have the courtesy to clean it up." He began to unclip the drape from around the table. "I'll make sure this gets changed before the panels start in here." He flipped the ends of the drape onto the table. Reaching down, he picked up a small item from under the table. In his hand lay a familiar flashy earring. Last seen on Dodie's ear the night before, it twinkled like a joke as the light hit it.

Leo tossed it on the table and ruefully regarded his pants, which now sported a smeared stain to match the one on the drape. "Now I need a drink," he said firmly. "The only thing harder to get out than tomato juice is blood," he said, indicating the stain on his trousers.

"Club soda," Janey said with authority. "That'll take care of whatever it is."

Korine reached out to pick up the earring. "I'll take this up to the room and put it with Dodie's things."

"Watch out!" Leo grabbed Korine's elbow, too late to keep her blouse from brushing against the stain on the drape. He jumped down beside Korine, cornering her between his body and the dais. Standing much too close for comfort, he brushed ineffectually at the stain on her sleeve, succeeding only in smearing it from elbow to wrist. If he hadn't had such a benevolent look on his face, Korine could have sworn he'd crowded her on purpose.

"Two club sodas," Korine said firmly. She pushed past Leo. "I've got one in the minibar in my room."

"Was that an offer?" Leo's lazy drawl caused a feeling akin to a hot flash as Korine realized how she had sounded. She could almost feel his eyes follow the flush as it traveled up her neck.

"I'm sure your room has a bottle too," she answered shortly.

Janey held the door open for everyone, then followed them through. On the other side of the door, Sharon stood with a pretty young woman with waist-length black hair, almost as if she were lying in wait for them.

"Have you seen Dodie?" Sharon's magnified eyes blinked at them solemnly from behind her bifocals. "She was scheduled to work in the Tropical Room during the first shift, but she never showed up."

Visions of Dodie's and Sharon's perfect coifs, topping jungle attire, flashed through Korine's head. Then she remembered. A local nursery which specialized in xeroscaping had "planted" a room with their products. Korine dragged her attention back from the ridiculous vision of Dodie in a sarong to realize that Leo had draped one arm around her shoulders.

Dismissing Sharon's sharp exclamation of concern when she spotted the red stain on Korine's blouse, Leo said, "Korine's simply the unfortunate victim of a rogue Bloody Mary."

Leo Gilcrest's first name was apt. The tone with which he spoke to Sharon could only be described as a growl. Korine's skin crawled where he had touched her. She shook off an unreasonable feeling of panic along with Leo's arm. She felt that he was using her to bait Sharon and, by extension, Dodie. She wasn't going to be a party to this game.

Casting a glare Leo's way that should leave him in no doubt as to what she thought of him, Korine stepped out of his reach and said to Sharon, "I'd be happy to check our room for you and see if Dodie's there."

"How about if I go with you," the young woman said, glancing at Sharon as if to get her permission. "That way I can show Dodie where the Tropical Room is if she's there. No sense in letting her get lost along the way, now, is there?"

With this rhetorical question, the young woman took Korine in hand and escorted her to the elevator. It didn't take two steps to discover that the young lady was Sharon's daughter, Holly.

Janey followed close behind the pair. "I'll go with you."

"No," Korine replied shortly, looking beyond Janey at Holly tapping her foot as she held the elevator door for Korine. "I'm going up to get some club soda out of that little refrigerator, change my clothes, and get ready to go out to Tybee Beach with Chaz. I don't want to discuss Leo Gilcrest anymore."

"I'll meet you down here later, then." Janey stopped and put a slim hand up to tuck a stray wavy lock behind her ear. She searched Korine's flushed face, then seemed to come to some conclusion. "It's okay, you know," Janey said. "Charlie's been dead a long time. I wasn't kidding earlier. You deserve to have someone nice."

Korine's mouth dried out, making it impossible to reply. Janey gave her an understanding look before walking away. Korine got on the elevator, automatically hitting the button for the fifth floor. Janey looked back over her shoulder, a half smile on her face. Behind Janey stood Leo Gilcrest, his arms crossed, an intense look on his face as he stared back at Korine. The doors slid closed, cutting off the view of the slow smile that spread over his face as he caught her watching him.

Nice, thought Korine, wresting her attention back to Holly, *is not at all the word I would use to describe Leo Gilcrest.*

THREE

THE BREEZE COMING IN off the water felt heavenly after the stifling heat of the city. Korine reached down and plucked her purse from the floorboard of the car, then slid out the open door. Chaz threw an enigmatic look at her from across the hood. Their car conversation, rather than providing Korine with the respite she needed, had gone from bad to worse.

It had begun with tales of Dodie and her antics, including the slightly surreal fight she'd overheard that morning. Her son had gotten a real kick out of the tale; obviously he wasn't rooming with the woman. Even though Chaz had laughed at Dodie's exploits, Korine still thought something was bothering him. She should have known better than to drag her nephew's name into the discussion. Chaz began to shut down right after she mentioned Dennis and Katie Anne.

From the time she'd taken in her nephew, there had been bad blood between the two boys. Neither Chaz nor Dennis would tell her what had happened to cause the rift. Whatever it was, it had widened last summer after Dennis got married.

Even after the tense exchange about Dennis and Ka-

tie Anne, Korine was unprepared for Chaz's sharp reaction when she asked if Richard and Leslie, his law
school friends, were going to settle down and start a
family soon. She didn't think it was all that tacky a
question—after all, they'd been living together since
college. Chaz had snapped out a negative answer to her
question. Stung by his unexpected anger, she'd turned
to the view outside the window for company. They'd
traveled the last few miles in silence.

"Chaz," Korine began, then stopped when he put his
arm around her shoulders and squeezed gently.

"I'm sorry, Mom. I shouldn't have taken this out on
you." He dropped his arm and took a step away from
her to look out over the waves while he continued.
"Richard and Leslie are breaking up. Things aren't going well, and Leslie's acting like a bitch. Settling down
and having a family is the last thing that they would do.
The whole thing is very painful."

Korine couldn't think of anything helpful to say to
ease his obvious distress. Unable to do more, she slid her
hand into his and they stood silent, surveying the roll-
ing surf. Her chest, aching in sympathy for Chaz's pain,
eased slowly as she looked down the sandy shoreline.

Tybee Beach looked like the town she'd grown up in.
Bait shops and small stores dotted the roadway between
weathered batten-board houses. It was a peaceful sort
of place. She could see why Chaz liked living here.

"They could sell this feeling wholesale," she said.

Chaz gave a short bark of laughter. "Don't let the de-
velopers hear you. So far we've avoided the high-rise,

overdevelopment dilemma that's ruined Florida beaches. I'm hoping that we will be able to do so indefinitely."

They walked a little way down the beach while they talked, and soon fetched up close to an old pier that stretched inland over a saltwater marsh.

Korine sighed, her tension abandoning her. The smell of the water, combined with the surrounding grasses, was as good as sharing a nice tall glass of tea and news of their daily lives with her friends. She smiled. Come to think of it, she was spending time with a friend. As if that moment of ease was tied up with the peaceful surroundings, she found herself wishing that she could move down here herself. She inhaled again and exhaled on a sigh. The heat was a bit much. She was glad that she had come, but moving wasn't in the cards.

Korine gave the hot sun a defiant look and started following the path along the dunes. She only half listened to Chaz's tale of one friend's rise in the law firm he'd joined in Washington, D.C., wondering instead what she could do to ease his frustration over Richard and Leslie.

Chaz had mentioned more than once that he wanted a relationship just like theirs. It was what kept alive her hope for grandchildren, despite the fact that Chaz was close to thirty and had shown no inclination to settle down.

While Korine had never met Leslie, she'd met Richard a few times during Chaz's law school days. The trio had been very close during school, and their friendship had endured.

She shook her head a little, trying to chase Chaz's

friends out of her brain. Richard and Leslie were replaced rapidly by images of Dodie and Leo. Korine had
managed to avoid Dodie altogether that morning, and
she had narrowly missed an encounter with Leo, avoid-
ing him through an expedient duck into the ladies' room
in the lobby. When she emerged, Chaz was there to pick
her up, and she escaped without further contact.

Her eyes crossed, trying to focus on the fingers waving in front of her face. She swatted Chaz's hand away.
"What was that for?" she demanded.

"Just checking to see if you were home."

Korine apologized but didn't explain. She wasn't
sure if she wanted to tell him that she was thinking of
a man when she should be hanging on her son's every
word. "Go on, you were talking about Stan?"

"I finished talking about Stan five minutes ago. I
knew you weren't listening." Chaz's voice held an un-
dertone of bitterness that Korine wasn't used to hearing.
Because they'd enjoyed such a good relationship for so
long, this was unsettling, to say the least.

"Try me again," she said softly. She looked up. As
soon as she made eye contact, she felt intuition shiver
up her spine. Something bigger than Richard and Leslie's relationship was troubling him. What on earth had
Chaz said that she'd missed? He turned away abruptly
and pointed the way back to the road. Like his father's,
Chaz's clear blue eyes always betrayed what he was
thinking. It made them lousy poker players, but it made
it easier for Korine to know when she was needed.

He turned and walked away instead of responding.

Staring at her son's retreating back, Korine wondered how she'd managed to miss hearing something that was obviously important to Chaz. She took a couple of half-running steps and caught up with him. She reached forward and plucked at his sleeve. "I really am sorry I was so inattentive. What were you saying?"

"Never mind. It's much too pretty a day for morbidly serious discussions. We'll talk about it some other time." Chaz turned, distracted by the flight of a great white pelican off to his left. The bird dove and rose again, a struggling fish in its beak.

Korine watched the pelican until it disappeared. It didn't leave any inspiration in its wake. Chaz had wandered away from her. He stood next to a clump of pampas grass, escaped from someone's yard and let loose upon the world. He turned and faced his mother as she approached.

The impression that something was terribly wrong grew with every step Korine took. Respecting his request to wait for another time was difficult. He'd never had trouble talking to her before. She wondered why he had it now. Mentally she ran down the list of possibilities. None of them seemed good.

Korine put one arm around her son, and they turned and walked back up to the road. Overlooking the dunes was an old silvered teak bench. Silently, they sat, neither of them settling back in their seats.

"I'm paying attention now," Korine began. She was interrupted by the roar of a Mustang convertible, carrying way too many teenagers, zooming past on the road behind them.

Chaz began to laugh. It wasn't the kind of laughing that made her want to join in, however. Ignoring the traffic behind her, she leaned over and folded her arms around her son. He continued to shake, but Korine knew that his laughter had turned to tears.

"Oh, Chaz," she whispered and thought he heard not only her words, but the cherished love she felt for him. His arms crept around her, and he leaned on her shoulder, reminding her of the way he used to hide his face in her shoulder when he was a little boy and had fallen and skinned his knee. She stroked the downy hair at the back of his neck and felt him slowly begin to relax.

The noise of the road receded as Korine's senses filled with images of Chaz growing up. She couldn't begin to imagine what was so wrong that he would act this way. Whatever was troubling him, they would face it, together, as they always had. He raised his head and looked into her eyes.

"You have cancer," Korine said, sure in the knowledge that Chaz was dying. His eyes had that bruised and frightened look that her husband's had held the day Charlie came home from Doc James's with his bad news.

"No, Mother, I'm perfectly healthy—" Chaz began.

"Korine McFaile." A familiar, deep voice rang out behind Korine, interrupting Chaz. "I never thought that you'd be one to rob the cradle."

Dear, sweet heaven, Korine thought. *How on earth did Leo Gilcrest find me?* She cast a furious look his way, then tightened her grip on her son, who was trying to stand. "Oh no you don't, Chaz," she said. "I'm not letting you get away from me until you tell me what is going on."

Chaz shrugged her off anyway and stood. "I don't think I've had the pleasure," he ground out, his jaw chiseled by clenched muscles. He extended his hand to the man.

"Leo Gilcrest. And you are?" The two men went through the ritual male handshake, each one trying to impress the other with the power of his grip.

"Chaz McFaile, Korine's son."

"You don't say." Leo's face eased.

Chaz, however, remained guarded. "You're the one…." The remainder of his sentence was drowned out by the return of the Mustang. The trio turned to watch as the tanned and boisterous young folk passed.

"The one what?" Leo asked, his face a study in amusement and interest.

"The one who got Dodie to settle down last night," Korine interjected.

Neither of the men paid the least bit of attention to her.

"You favor Korine," Leo said.

Chaz raised one eyebrow. "I'm told I look like my father," he replied.

Korine slipped her arm through Chaz's and said, "Sweetheart, I am positively dying of thirst. Could you run and get me some iced tea from that shop over there?"

Chaz broke eye contact with Leo long enough to stare incredulously down at his mother. She put on her best just-do-it look, and Chaz, unbelievably, obeyed.

As soon as her son was out of earshot, Korine said,

"I thought I'd made myself clear this morning. Stick to Dodie, I'm not interested."

"In what?" Leo raised an eyebrow of his own as he looked down at her.

His voice lapped at her senses. She blinked and clenched a fist, sticking her nails firmly into the palm of her hand. It was not the time or the place, not to mention the company, in which to indulge her sense of loss.

Despite her firm intentions, Korine found her eyes burning. "Just leave me alone!" she said in a low voice. For a moment, she felt her control slip. Pain flashed through her with an intensity that left her shaking. Turning, she walked rapidly away.

It had taken her so long to regain her self-composure. Why did this man have to turn up now and steal it away from her? Stumbling over a stone by the side of the road, she put a hand out to brace herself against the road sign next to her. She threw a glance over her shoulder and found Leo Gilcrest staring after her. The bewildered expression on his face gave her no satisfaction.

She jumped when Chaz put his hand on her shoulder. He'd come up on her from behind and must have seen a goodly portion of that exchange. His expression was carefully neutral, something for which Korine was devoutly grateful.

Her relief was short-lived. Chaz's next words rocked her further. "We've got to get back to the hotel. I just heard a report on the radio in there." He indicated the shop behind him with a nod of his head. "Your roommate won't be bothering you anymore. Dodie Halloran was found dead, just after lunch."

Korine did the only thing open to her under the circumstances. She burst into tears. As Chaz fished in his pocket for a handkerchief, the noise of the young people greeting each other from their open car windows roared in Korine's ears, mocking her with their cheerfulness.

By the time she finished blowing her nose and had gathered enough self-control to look around, Leo Gilcrest had vanished. Korine didn't ask Chaz if Leo had overheard the news about Dodie. He wasn't her concern.

FOUR

With regret, J.J. watched the credits roll for the "Bonanza" episode on the TV sitting on the counter at the coffee shop. He didn't have cable at home, so he hadn't realized what he was missing. He'd have to talk with Janey and see if they could squeeze it into their budget. Gathering his coffee things together, he pitched them in the trash can. He'd gone out for some fresh air along with his breakfast over two hours earlier. Janey would be wondering what hole he had fallen into.

Strolling down the tree-shaded street, J.J. wondered again how Janey had brought herself up so far, so fast. Even a year ago, she'd still experienced occasional "spells" if J.J. got angry. She hadn't suffered a panic attack since last summer, and he intended that she never would again. He picked a blossom off a camellia shrub. It would be just the thing to use to distract her if she was worried about him.

Pushing through the revolving doors, J.J. entered the hotel lobby. He looked at his watch. Nine thirty. Janey would either be in a conference room or in the restaurant off the lobby, having a cup of coffee with someone. Sure enough, the first smiling face he saw in the restaurant was Janey's.

"Should have known you'd find someone interesting to talk to. Do you mind if I join you?" J.J. asked.

Janey looked delighted to see him. Her companion, a young dark-haired woman of about twenty, was less so. "Where have you been?" Janey exclaimed. "I've been looking all over for you."

He felt a little sheepish telling her where he'd been all that time, so he said, "There's a coffee shop around the corner. I was reading the paper and lost track of the time." He handed the creamy yellow camellia blossom to his wife. She breathed in its sweet fragrance while J.J. pulled out a chair and sat down. Janey introduced him to the young woman, Sharon's daughter, Holly. He wasn't sure why the girl left him feeling cold; Janey obviously liked her.

"Davidson," Holly said in response to Janey's question about where she went to school. "I came down this weekend to help Mom with this conference. Not," she added, "that Mom would actually let me do anything." Holly smiled tightly, as if trying to convince herself that she hadn't sounded petulant.

"Where's Korine?" J.J. asked.

"She and Chaz went to the beach," Janey answered. "She said they'd be back in time for lunch."

Holly placed her folded napkin on the table and stood. "I'd better go see if I can track down Dodie before Mom finds her. Neither of them is up to any more fireworks like last night."

J.J. waited until Holly had left the restaurant before speaking. "Is it just me, or is that one crazy, mixed-up family?"

Janey answered slowly, her face still turned as if watching the girl, even though she was out of sight. "Apparently, Dodie comes to visit them once a month or more. She and Sharon are close."

"My family's close," J.J. said. "I don't know if I would want them in my house that often."

Janey swiveled in her seat and faced J.J. "Dodie fancies herself as a fairy godmother for Holly. Can you imagine what that child's life must be like, caught between those two women all the time?"

"What do you mean?" J.J. asked.

"Dodie's the one who's paying for Holly's schooling. Sharon wanted her to stay at home and go to the community college. They've evidently got a decent enough botany program." Janey stopped and looked at her husband.

"What?" he asked.

"You're not listening."

"Well, now that you mention it, I was thinking that I might run over to the Maritime Museum for a couple of hours, then meet you back here for lunch."

"You *weren't* listening!" Janey's voice became indignant.

"Yes, I was. But I really can't understand why you find it so fascinating to discover all these little details about a total stranger's life."

"That's how we become friends."

"Even if, beyond all reason, you became friends with either one of those women, I would not want them darkening our door. Dodie and Sharon simply aren't nice people." J.J. felt his temperature rising, and he made an effort to calm down.

"I see," Janey said ominously. "You aren't listening to me because you don't care if these women interest me or not."

J.J. stared at his wife. She had gone from fragile flower to fighting machine in one short year. He wasn't sure he was going to be ready for her if this transition kept up. He did know that he'd better apologize, even if he didn't know what it was that he'd done wrong. "I'm sorry," he said.

Janey's face eased slightly. "We need to talk," she said.

J.J. wondered what the heck he'd said. She had never sounded so intense in all the time he'd known her. He tossed enough money on the table to cover the meal and got up.

Janey refused to discuss whatever was on her mind until after they'd exited the elevators and had gained the privacy of their room. By that time, J.J. was convinced that Janey was going to ask him for a divorce—or something worse, although he couldn't imagine anything worse than losing her.

Once the door closed behind them and they were alone, J.J. said, "What's going on?"

"Sharon miscarried three times before Holly was born. I don't think I can take that."

J.J. held his breath while Janey started crying. He released it when she allowed him to fold his arms around her instead of fighting him off, as she had so often done in the past. This was genuine fear and grief, not a delayed panic attack.

"We don't have to have children." Even as J.J. spoke, he felt a lump form in his throat.

"No!" Janey's response ripped the air. She pushed J.J. away and stood in front of him, fists balled and raised as if to fight off the notion that they would not have children. He'd known it was important to her, but he hadn't realized just how deep-seated her need was.

Janey stood, her shoulders square. "I want children. I'll love them whether I birth them, or if they come fully formed. My preference is to carry your children and raise them to be as wonderful as their daddy." She took a step closer and wiped a tear from J.J.'s cheek. "It scares me to death to think about losing them over and over again, but I don't want to stop trying."

J.J. pulled his wife to him. Her head fit perfectly in the hollow of his shoulder. He could feel the warmth of her through his polo shirt. Running his finger lightly over her own fine features, he found a tear or two tracing their way down new worry lines. He tipped her head. Kissing her felt like a heartfelt prayer.

Lifting heavy eyelids, J.J. looked deep into Janey's doe-brown eyes. "Just because you lost one, doesn't mean you'll lose another. I'd like a child with you. But I don't love you for the children you'll bear. I love you because you are the prettiest, most awe-inspiring woman I've ever met."

She stretched up to greet his lips with a kiss so searing, J.J. knew he'd said the right thing. Smiling, he looked steadily at Janey, then tossed her on the bed. Laughing at her mock-outraged expression, he joined her.

THE PHONE WOKE J.J. up. The shower was running in the bathroom. He crawled across the bed to snatch the phone off the hook. He dropped the receiver on the floor. In trying to pick it up, he slid off the bed, landing on his tailbone. Wrapping the fallen sheet around his dignity, he picked up the phone.

"Hello," J.J. said cautiously.

"Is Korine McFaile there, please?"

"Wrong room. Call the operator and ask her to transfer you to room 555." J.J. started to hang up, but the man continued to talk, so he put the phone back to his ear. He caught the tail end of a sentence: "…discuss the death of her roommate, Dodie Halloran."

J.J. said, "Dodie Halloran's dead?" Mind racing, he went over the possibilities and came up with one very ugly picture.

"Mr. Bascom, I need to reach your friend Mrs. McFaile. Mrs. Winslow said you might know where I could find her."

"Who is this?" J.J. asked, even though he pretty much already knew.

"Detective Sudley. Savannah Police Department."

Damn, J.J. thought, rubbing his scalp with one hand. That ugly picture was coming more clearly into focus. "I ought to tell you now," he said, "I'm Chief of Police back home."

The reply on the other end was, if possible, even colder than the initial tone with which Sudley had asked for Korine.

"How do I reach you if I track down Korine before

you do?" J.J. asked. He scribbled the number down on the pad on the bedside table. Giving Sudley his assurance that he would call him as soon as he found Korine, he hung up.

Janey came out of the bathroom, rubbing her hair with a towel. "Who was it?" she asked.

J.J. hauled himself up off the floor and tossed the bedcovers back on the mattress. Heading for the bathroom, he paused next to Janey and laid his hands gently on her shoulders. "Dodie Halloran's been killed. That was the police officer who's assigned to her case. They're looking for Korine."

"They don't think—" Janey couldn't finish that thought out loud.

"They'll think a lot of things before they're through," J.J. answered. He put one hand out and rubbed Janey's shoulder. She took the news pretty well. She hadn't heard Sudley's tone of voice when he said Korine's name.

"Right now," J.J. said, "I'm going to get dressed and get out there and do some looking of my own."

"I'll come too," Janey said, pulling open a drawer and selecting clothes.

"I'd rather you didn't."

Janey's back stiffened. She turned around. "They do think Korine had something to do with this, don't they?"

"It's possible," J.J. equivocated. "I don't want you getting in the middle of this investigation. Sudley isn't me. He'll throw you in jail if you try the stunts you and Korine pulled last summer. I don't want that to happen."

"I didn't pull any stunts," Janey began.

"Korine did. Please, just stay out of it." J.J. said this with as much finality as he dared put into his tone of voice.

Janey stared at him, then turned her back and pulled her shirt on over her head. "Is it permissible for me to look for Korine?"

J.J. stalked over and stood in front of Janey. "Honey, don't take it that way. I don't want you hurt. Dodie was murdered. Whoever killed her might just kill somebody perceived as a threat. And anyone poking around is a threat."

"Does that include you?"

"I'm a trained police officer. Yes, I could be targeted, but I'm far less likely to become a victim than you are." J.J. grinned suddenly. "I promise to share information with you if you'll let me do the digging."

Janey reluctantly grinned back. "Sharing is good for a relationship. But don't make this local guy mad because you're treading on his toes. I don't want to see you in jail— or dead—any more than you want to see me that way."

"Gotcha," J.J. said.

It wasn't until he heard the door slam after Janey as he stood in the shower that J.J. realized she hadn't given him any promises at all. He flipped off the water and stepped out onto the cold tile. Reaching for a towel, he chastised himself. When was he ever going to learn?

WHEN J.J. GOT to the lobby, the first thing he saw was a cluster of uniformed officers by the front desk talking to a tall man in plain clothes. He was either a suspect or the detective investigating the case. J.J. headed on over.

"Sudley?" J.J. inquired.

The man turned cool gray eyes on J.J. and lifted an eyebrow. "Yes?" he answered shortly.

J.J. stuck his hand out. "J.J. Bascom. We spoke on the phone a short while ago."

Sudley transferred the driving hat he held to his other hand and grasped J.J.'s proffered hand. "Have you found Mrs. McFaile yet?"

"She's still out with her son," J.J. replied. At least he assumed so. He wanted to get some information from Sudley about why he wanted Korine so badly before he pointed anyone in her direction. Sizing the man up, J.J. decided he looked intelligent enough. "What happened to Dodie?"

"I'm really not at liberty to speak about the case yet," the detective replied.

J.J. carefully kept his face blank. He hadn't expected Sudley to fall all over himself, but J.J. would have been more courteous than this to a fellow officer, had the circumstances been reversed.

Sudley shot J.J. a keen look from under his bushy eyebrows and said, "I realize that you're used to being in the middle of things, but this is not your town, and it would be most helpful if you'd leave this to us." His tone made it very clear what he thought of a small-town policeman's abilities.

J.J.'s estimation of the man plummeted. He didn't have any expectations of being offered anything more than professional courtesy. This wasn't it. "Do you mind telling me what it is that you want with Korine?"

"Good friend of yours?" Sudley asked.

"Very good friend." J.J. kept his answer short.

"I need to ask her some questions. It's early yet to be coming to any conclusions." Sudley had not come out and said that he suspected Korine, but he'd sure intimated it.

Who has Sudley been speaking with so far? J.J. wondered. Despite the detective's words, he might have already made up his mind about Korine before he even met her. Initially, J.J. hadn't been panting to investigate. But, pretty much having been told to mind his own business because his friend might be involved was like a pebble in his shoe. He knew that the irritation would get worse if he didn't do something about it.

He treated Sudley to a taste of his own medicine and gave him a look that should have left the man in no doubt that

J.J. had a vital interest in the case.

Sudley's body stiffened; he had gotten the message loud and clear. And Janey said men didn't pay attention to nonverbal communication.

With a feeling of unease, J.J. turned and left the group of policemen. Complying with Sudley's request would be easy if Korine weren't the one who seemed to be front and center in the investigation.

Going down one level, it didn't take his detective's training to discover where the body had been found. A still-hysterical housekeeper, white apron askew over her navy uniform, was pointing toward the service elevator while talking to an eager group of women.

J.J. pondered his course of action. On the one hand, he owed it to Sudley as a fellow police officer to stay out of it. On the other hand, it wouldn't hurt anyone if he kept his eyes and ears open for information. Just in case his intuition that Sudley suspected Korine was correct.

It wasn't as if he had tracked this woman down and was asking her for privileged facts; she was blurting them out to everyone who wandered by. J.J. couldn't help it if she'd already disclosed that she discovered the body around noon in a linen cart which contained the soiled linen from the banquet the night before. It had been left, forgotten, in the service hallway behind the conference area. She'd put some extra dirty linen in it, tried to roll it, hadn't been able to, moved a stained and rumpled table skirt, and screamed.

When she demonstrated this part to the avidly listening women, J.J. walked through them. "Ma'am," he said. "Didn't Detective Sudley ask you to keep this confidential?"

Remembering the snide look on Sudley's face as he told J.J. to stay out of things made resisting the opportunity futile. Shooing the onlookers away from the housekeeper's side, he said, "Tell me again how you came to find the victim."

"I came in and stripped the tablecloth off that table there." The woman paused to point at the crime-scene-tape-festooned door of one of the conference rooms. "Somebody had spilled stuff all over it, and they'd asked us to make sure we put clean on before they opened that room up." She looked up nervously at J.J.

"It was handy that the linen cart was out there for you to put those things into," he said, hoping to relax the woman.

"It was plain odd," she said.

"The cart looked odd?"

"No, it looked fine. But it shouldn't have been there. Wanda, my supervisor, is going to spit nails. She likes everything real neat and tidy. A full, dirty cart like that—it like to ruins our day, she gets so mean."

J.J. didn't mention what kind of mood her supervisor was going to enjoy, what with a dead body in a dirty cart that shouldn't have been there in the first place.

"Who can get back here?"

"Employees. The occasional lost hotel guest. But sure as my name's Roxanne Jackson, I can swear none of us did this. We didn't know her. For as bad a shape as she was in, she'd been tidied up a bit before they tucked her in that basket. Who would bother to do that, if you don't know her and care about her? Poor thing, lying there, curled up like a puppy, but all funny colored and unsettled looking. She must have fought back. Poor thing had a horrible bruise on her cheek, and only the one earring on."

"What wounds did she have? Tidied up how?" he asked intently.

Suspicion dawned on the housekeeper's face. "Who did you say you were?"

J.J. tried to find something innocent but compelling

to say that would make him sound official without actually sounding like he was representing himself that way. It took too long.

The woman stood up. "I'm no fool. You told me not to talk with those women so I'd talk to you." Her lined face registered fear. "How do I know you aren't the one who killed her?"

"If I killed her, I wouldn't need to ask you about her wounds. A friend of mine was the victim's roommate here in the hotel."

The housekeeper looked mollified but didn't quite step over that line into trust. She crossed her arms across her chest. "I don't think I'd better talk to you anymore."

J.J. gave her the steady look he gave witnesses back home who weren't cooperating. "I quite understand. I'm asking these questions because I know that my friend couldn't have done this." He wrote his name and room number on a slip of paper and gave it to the woman. "Think about it. An innocent woman might wind up in jail."

That point sank home, and she pocketed the slip of paper. J.J. knew she might throw it away later, but he had her name, where she worked, and probably most of the valuable information she'd given Sudley.

Thoughtfully, he watched the housekeeper disappear into the service hallway. J.J. turned and took the steps in search of his wife. He had a promise to extract.

FIVE

WHEN CHAZ AND KORINE reached the hotel, the people in the lobby were going about the business of conferencing as usual. After her initial reaction, Korine realized that, to people who didn't know Dodie, her death was only one more morsel of gossip to pass around and chew on before going home.

Chaz went to find J.J. and Janey while Korine checked in at the desk in the lobby. She wasn't naïve enough to think that she'd be allowed to return to her room.

"Mrs. McFaile?" The desk clerk's voice cracked. He was the one who had tried to help her find another room that morning. "Detective Sudley asked if you could wait over there for him. I'll let him know you're back." His eyes were round. Korine warmed to the nice young man. Obviously, murder wasn't business as usual to him.

"Thank you, Javier," she replied. It wasn't until she'd sat down under the potted palms in the corner that Korine realized that he was nervous because of her, not the murder. Crossing her arms over her chest, she stared at the palm tree next to her. She needed some time to think.

She didn't get it.

Sharon Winslow exited the elevator. Face swollen

and tearful, she made a beeline for Korine as if she'd known exactly where she was sitting.

"How could you!" Sharon hissed. Korine was reminded forcibly of Dodie's red face the night before. There was a very strong family resemblance.

Figuring out what Sharon meant didn't take a lot of brainpower. Figuring out what to say did. Unfortunately, after the events of the day, Korine wasn't as facile as she would have liked to have been.

"Dodie didn't deserve this!" Sharon's voice was rising.

"No, she didn't," Korine agreed. She even found a tear falling from her eye as she said it, which threw Sharon so much that she plopped heavily into the next chair and stared at Korine. Mustering as much tact as she could under the circumstances, Korine said, "I'm sorry about Dodie, really I am."

"But you didn't even like her," Sharon said, her anger gone. Her plump cheeks sagged under the weight of her grief. Behind her glasses, her round eyes blinked rapidly, fighting back tears.

"No," Korine admitted finally, deciding that dissembling wouldn't be productive. "I didn't like Dodie. But I would have been free of her after the weekend. Why kill her over a few days' discomfort?"

Sharon's eyes narrowed. "But then Leo Gilcrest came into the picture, didn't he?"

Korine was not going to sit there and let Sharon insinuate that she was a flirt. She stood up. In as cold a tone as she had ever used, Korine said, "You can take it from me that I have absolutely no designs upon

Leo Gilcrest." She turned on her heel, intending to walk away.

Instead, she ran into the solid wall of a man standing behind her. Tall, with thinning blond hair combed across his scalp, he held a battered, plaid driving cap in his hands. The aw-shucks expression on his face didn't jibe with the intelligence she saw deep within his gray eyes.

"Excuse me," she said.

"Actually, Mrs. McFaile, if I could have a few moments of your time." It was not a request.

Korine asked, "And you are?" She was acutely aware of Sharon standing on the other side of the coffee table.

"Detective Sudley." The policeman looked apologetic as he fished an ID badge out of his hip pocket and flashed it at her. "I couldn't help but hear your conversation."

Korine felt the blood drain from her face.

"Mrs. Winslow, if you'll excuse us for a moment?" The officer indicated that Korine should accompany him.

Even as she felt her knees quiver, Korine said, "If this is about Dodie, then perhaps we could wait here for my son. If you don't mind," she added after a brief but furious look crossed the man's face.

Korine sat down on the edge of one of the chairs. Looking up, she saw Sudley's features settle into a carefully neutral mask. Had he really thought that she would trot off with him? She knew that if she was a suspect, she surely wasn't first on the list. Even so, Sudley wasn't a friend, as J.J. was. Korine wasn't about to talk with him until she had some support from someone she knew she could trust.

Sharon looked uncertainly from one of them to the other, then said hesitantly, "I think I'll be going."

The officer smiled at her. "You've been very helpful, Mrs. Winslow. I'm sure you have lots to do. I'll find you later if I need to."

She walked away, glancing over her shoulder at the pair of them standing there beside the table.

"Do you mind if we wait in the restaurant?" Sudley asked.

"Actually," Korine answered, "that sounds like a good idea."

He flourished his hat with his hand, indicating that he would follow Korine. As she passed him, he closed in behind her. The old-fashioned gesture didn't feel mannerly; it felt more like he'd just established his superiority.

With a good bit of trepidation, Korine took her chair. Sudley waited until she was settled before being seated himself. Again, the exaggerated dance of manners made her uneasy rather than making her feel at home. The waitress brought them both coffee, and Korine doctored hers with two packets of sugar. If she was any judge of character, she was going to need the extra energy.

"How long have you been in the landscaping business?" Sudley asked.

Korine looked sourly at him across the top of her coffee mug. She took a sip before she answered. "Professionally? A year. As an enthusiast, I think pretty much forever."

Sudley gave her a sidelong glance. "I'd appreciate your help in establishing some things about Mrs. Halloran. Are you up to talking now, or do you still want to wait for your son?"

Korine considered, then said, "I really didn't know her all that well. Sharon put us in the same room because she thought we ought to get to know one another better—Dodie had recently moved up to my neck of the woods."

"And you didn't get on."

Korine put her cup down on the table. "If you've talked to Sharon, you know we didn't. Dodie went out of her way to make me unhappy about rooming with her. I don't know why. I know that makes me look bad, since she's been murdered. But I'm not going to lie and tell you we were friends. I'd seen enough to know I didn't ever need to be around her again; but as I pointed out to Sharon, that's not grounds for murder."

Sudley looked at her reproachfully. "Did I ask if you killed her?"

Korine didn't dignify his question with an answer. It was strange. She felt that Sudley was enjoying her discomfiture. She'd heard of policemen playing Good Cop/Bad Cop. She hoped that the Good Cop would arrive soon. She didn't like this one a bit.

Sudley pulled out a small tape recorder and placed it on the table in front of Korine. A couple of conference-goers passed the table and did a double take when they heard the officer give Korine the official warning that their conversation was being recorded and would become evidence.

Korine felt naked. She wished they'd gone somewhere more private so that she could be spared this public indignity. To her relief, she saw Chaz step off the elevator and come in their direction.

She performed the introductions. Sudley rose and the two men shook hands briefly. Chaz's brows drew together as he pulled out the chair to Korine's right and sat down. Obviously, he didn't like Sudley any more than she did.

"Your mother was just helping me establish what has happened so far this weekend," Sudley said.

Korine knew she looked harassed, even though the detective's questions had been innocuous. Chaz turned a sharp eye on the man. "What do you have so far?" he asked.

It was Sudley's turn to look harassed. "We're looking into several possibilities."

"In other words, you're fishing. Surely you have someone out there with a better motive—not to mention opportunity—to have killed Dodie," Chaz said dryly.

"Actually, we're estimating time of death to be between nine and ten this morning."

"That would have been about the time—" Korine broke off at Chaz's look.

"About the time what?" Sudley's tone was whip sharp.

"I haven't had a chance to tell Mother that a friend of mine is on his way. Richard Colthurst."

Sudley obviously knew Richard by reputation, if not in person. His eyebrows rose.

Korine knew Chaz was sending her a warning. She had already gotten that message from Sudley's manner.

"I don't have anything to hide." She directed this at Chaz, who sighed, leaned back, and waved his hands in the air, as if warding off all responsibility for her actions.

"I have to look at everything," Sudley said. Flipping open a pad to take notes in addition to the recording, he prepared to get down to business. "Can you run through what you've done so far this weekend?"

At Chaz's reluctant nod, Korine began again with meeting Sharon at registration where she learned that she would be rooming with Dodie. Even though true, Korine realized how lame her story sounded. She had never met Dodie face to face, but they didn't live all that far apart. She admitted to having had misgivings about rooming with Dodie. Korine hadn't said anything at the time because Sharon was obviously at her wit's end trying to see to everything for the conference. Korine felt it wouldn't be necessary to impose on her by asking her to reassign roommates.

It didn't take long to describe the comments that Dodie had leveled at Korine while she was unpacking, or the miscommunication between Sharon, Korine, and Dodie the night before. Leo's name stuck in Korine's throat when she explained how she and Dodie had finally made their peace before they had retired to the privacy of their room. She even put in that Dodie's snoring had kept her awake.

When Korine got to the part about the PA broadcast of Dodie's argument from the next room, Sudley leaned forward. "Who was she arguing with?" he asked.

"I don't know," Korine answered truthfully. She suspected that it had been Leo, but she wasn't about to bring up his name again.

"Could it have been the same person you overheard her arguing with when you were in the shower?" Chaz suggested.

That hadn't even occurred to Korine. "Perhaps," she said, then she frowned. "Dodie said that the person she argued with in our room was a friend of mine."

"And that might be…?" Sudley prompted.

Korine shook her head. "I don't know," she lied. From the swift glance that Chaz sent her way, she knew that he had caught her hesitation.

"Go on," Sudley said, looking up from his notes. Korine nearly sighed with relief. He'd missed Chaz's look while scribbling down what she'd said.

She recited the rest of the events of the day. Resuming her story with the earring that they had found under the table on the platform, Korine included the totally uninteresting conversation that she and Holly had enjoyed on the elevator ride up to her room, finishing with the news story that Chaz had heard on the radio out at Tybee Beach.

Sudley was a good listener, keeping his eyes on her face and asking for more information when she left out who else had been around. It was disquieting how often he recognized when she'd left something out.

Finally, he flipped his notebook shut and shoved it back into his pocket. Korine allowed herself a brief sigh of relief as she took a sip of her tepid coffee. That relief seemed short-lived when Sudley signaled the waitress to come fill up his cup.

Interestingly, the detective's next question was aimed at Chaz. "So you've moved down here to our city. What's impressed you the most so far?"

"The heat," Chaz answered shortly. He smiled to soften his tone. "I lived down here for a while, interning during law school. Moved back down here a few months ago."

"Nice that your mom could come down and y'all could get in a visit."

Chaz agreed amiably. He and Korine exchanged glances. Sudley's attempts to establish himself as congenial and just-folks were heavy-handed.

"Anything you want to add to your momma's story?" Sudley asked suddenly, breaking their silent communication.

"Not a thing." Chaz settled back in his chair and drained his coffee mug.

"Mrs. Winslow had quite a bit to say about you," Sudley said, turning back to Korine. "She seemed to think that you and Ms. Halloran were rivals."

"Dodie had recently put an ad in the paper in Pine Grove looking for people to use her landscaping service. It was no skin off my nose. We have more business than we can comfortably carry. I wouldn't call us rivals," Korine answered. She didn't like the tone of voice that Sudley used.

He looked steadily at Korine. "I didn't realize that you were business rivals too," he said.

Chaz gave his mother an inquiring look.

Korine knew she'd fallen into that one. Rather than

make the same mistake twice, she didn't respond to Sudley's gambit.

After a moment passed, during which time Sudley seemed content to wait Korine out, Chaz spoke. "Do I need to caution Mother to wait until Richard gets here to answer any more questions?" he asked.

"If you feel it would be best for her to wait for your lawyer friend," Sudley countered. He turned to look Korine directly in the eye as he added, "You and I both know that you had more at stake here than roommate squabbles." He set his coffee down on the table, leaned back, and waited.

Korine swallowed, having trouble getting past the lump in her throat. She wondered if anyone was paying attention to her when she said that she didn't have an interest in Leo Gilcrest. "You're referring to Leo; and no, we are not—nor will we ever be—an item. I don't know what the nature of his relationship with Dodie was, but the two of us didn't even know each other, much less have a relationship."

"I'll make sure and tell Mr. Gilcrest that when I see him. He's the next one on my list of people to track down and talk with. You wouldn't happen to know where I could find him, would you?"

"No," Korine ground out. "I don't have a clue about where he might be. You could always try picking up the phone and calling his room."

"Speaking of which," Chaz interrupted, "if you're finished, Mother was wondering when she could collect her things."

Sudley traced a finger through a bead of spilled water on the table in front of him. "Mrs. Winslow was able to help us identify which items belonged to the victim. I can have one of the men round up everything else for you, if you like."

Korine felt something twist inside at Sudley's dismissive referral to Dodie. *The victim.* The phrase brought up a vividly horrid mental image. It was on the tip of her tongue to ask how Dodie had died when Korine decided that she really didn't want to know. She shivered. Someone had murdered Dodie, someone that she had talked with, perhaps even traded jokes with, in the last day or so.

She looked up to find Sudley watching her, startled to glimpse what looked like compassion in his odd gray eyes. Whatever it was, it didn't last long.

"Let me know where you wind up staying, and we'll deliver your things to you there," Sudley said. "I'm not sure if they can find you a room here in the hotel or if you'll go home with your son. If all else fails, there are several hotels in the area."

Korine nodded and stood. She hooked her pocketbook over her shoulder and let Chaz take her arm as they went to check with the desk clerk to see if there was anything that he could do for her. She appreciated the black humor in her situation. Alive, Dodie had done her level best to make Korine's life miserable. Ironically, by dying, she achieved that very goal.

SIX

KORINE PUSHED OPEN the door to her new room and gasped. The desk clerk and the shift supervisor had felt so sorry for her by the time Chaz had finished with them, that they bumped one of their late arrivals to free up a room for her. And what a room.

On the top floor of the hotel, the room could be nothing other than the bridal suite. As Korine took it in, her purse fell from her hand. Chaz came in behind her and shut the door, plucking the bag off the floor and giving her a mock push with the tips of his fingers.

"The room's adequate, don't you think?" Chaz's voice was amused. Korine had kicked off her tennis shoes and wiggled her toes deep into the plush pink carpet.

"Dodie would have loved this," Korine said, sobering. She slid into one of a pair of rainbow-colored chenille armchairs by the window and looked out over the city.

"I never met the woman, but the feeling I get is that nothing would have made her happy. She ruined your vacation, and then she died. I don't want to hear another word about her."

"No one is so completely horrible that you shouldn't

mourn her death," she said. She hugged herself. It was cold, thinking about Dodie lying there. Had she died slowly? Had she been afraid? Shivering, Korine tucked one leg up under her and nestled closer into the chair.

"I didn't say she deserved to die," Chaz responded. "I've got to worry about whether or not you're going to wind up with the blame for her death, that's all."

"We heard her arguing with her murderer." Korine shot up out of her chair and prowled around the luxurious room. "While the speaker was going on about roses, of all things," she said.

Chaz came over and stood in Korine's path, effectively stopping her pacing. "You couldn't have prevented this any more than you would have killed her yourself. Dodie's dead. There's not a damn thing you can do about that now."

The phone rang on the table at Korine's elbow. Rather than responding to Chaz's unanswerable statement, she picked up the receiver. "Hello?"

Janey's voice came over the line. "Finally! We've been trying to find you ever since we heard what happened."

"We just got in," Korine said. "Chaz is here with me."

"He came back with you," Janey said, sounding relieved. "Is there anything we can do?"

Korine covered the mouthpiece with one hand and repeated the offer to Chaz.

"Food" was his reply. To her surprise, Korine's stomach rumbled, announcing its second to Chaz's request.

Korine spoke to Janey again. "Come up and bring something to eat. We missed lunch, and we're hungry."

"Done. Wait, J.J. wants a turn."

A few fumbling noises later, J.J.'s voice came over the line. "Did the detective find you?"

"Sudley? Yes, I spoke with him. Is he as stupid as he seems?"

"I doubt it. Stupid people don't get to detective rank. Who was with you when you talked to him?"

"Chaz was there."

"Good. Chaz is probably in his element with murder around."

"J.J.!" Korine protested. She was appalled to find a chuckle emerging from her throat. Chaz had always liked conflict. J.J. was right; her son looked far better now than he had all day.

"Good, you laughed," he replied. "We'll be up as soon as we rustle up some food."

Korine hung up the phone. She sat back down and gazed out over the city. Savannah was beautiful from the ground. Seen from ten stories up, the lush green vegetation of the city made it look almost tropical. She stole a look at Chaz, who sat, hands clasped over his stomach. His mind seemed very far removed from the view just outside the window.

"Penny for them?" Korine asked.

"What?" Chaz asked. "Oh, nothing in particular. It's been a hell of a day." He leaned forward and rose from the chair. Going over to the window, he placed one palm against the windowpane and rested his head against it.

"Is now a good time to talk?" Korine asked. Events

had delayed their earlier conversation, but she didn't want him to think she'd forgotten.

"You don't want my advice," Chaz said wryly, drawing circles on the glass with his forefinger. "It's a good thing I asked Richard to stop by. You'll do better to ask him. I'll spend way too much time worrying about you to be of any help."

Exasperated, Korine got up and went to face her son. She reached out and grabbed his hand away from the window. Startled, he looked down at her.

"I'm listening now," she said softly.

Chaz tore his hand away. "Oh, for heaven's sake, Mother, don't be so melodramatic."

"It sounded important this morning."

"I was talking about Richard and Leslie."

"I see," Korine said, although she didn't. There were undertones to her son's statement, things she couldn't identify. "If Richard is going to be here," she said, "then maybe you'll fill me in again on what's going on between him and Leslie. I don't want to step on any sensitive toes."

Chaz turned his face slightly away from her. His profile stood out in relief against the light behind him. He had his father's stubborn little chin.

"Please? He's your friend, and I don't want to hurt him."

Chaz turned back to her. His voice was harsh when he said, "Richard left Leslie because he's found somebody else."

Taken aback by her son's harsh tone, Korine said,

"And you don't approve?" When he turned his face away from her, Korine grew even more confused. "Well, I'll watch what I say around him. Do you know the other party?"

"Yes, I know the other 'party.'" He bit off the word.

Korine reached out and slid her arm around Chaz's waist. His back was tense as stone. With an exclamation, he rocketed away from her comforting embrace and went to answer a knock at the door.

J.J. and Janey trooped in, carrying several large bags. The sweet scent of delicately spiced dishes made Korine's mouth water. Janey took one look at the decor and darted into the bedroom. Whoops of laughter emerged.

Korine went in to see what she found so funny. In the center of the room—spotlight, mirrors, and all—was a large heart-shaped, red-covered bed. She was speechless. When they'd come in earlier, she hadn't gotten any farther than the chairs in the room outside before collapsing. Exploring the bedroom had been the last thing on her mind. She found her voice. "Would you like to trade rooms?"

"Oh, no. I don't think I want J.J. to have a coronary. You keep it."

"Thanks, I think."

After J.J. and Chaz had joined the women to see what all the fuss was about, they all settled down around a mahogany card table next to the wet bar. As he pulled one carton after another out of the brown paper sack he had carried in, J.J. pronounced the names of Korine's favorite Chinese dishes. It didn't take long before they were digging into plates mounded high with the delicious food.

J.J. related that he had talked with the startled housekeeper who had discovered Dodie's body. "Stuffed under a bunch of wadded-up old napkins in a linen cart," J.J. said. "She looked like hell."

Janey grimaced.

Korine felt sick to her stomach. She put her fork down next to her plate.

J.J. turned to Janey as soon as he finished speaking. He took her hand and apologized for his language. "Sweetheart, I'm sorry. But she was dead. It wasn't one of her better days."

Korine turned pea green. "How can you talk about her like that? It's not funny!"

J.J. looked at Korine contritely. "I'm sorry. You're right. I make jokes on the job to deal with the horrible things. Not appropriate in the present company."

He stood up and moved over to sit with Chaz by the window. Their murmured conversation continued to hash out the possibilities of Dodie's death, but this time J.J. held off on the macabre jokes. Korine tried not to listen as J.J. filled Chaz in on his discussion with the poor woman who had discovered Dodie's dead body.

After Chaz finished reciting the interview that Sudley had subjected Korine to, J.J. looked steadily over at her. J.J. said, loudly enough for Korine to catch every word, "Korine's going to be on the short list. If someone Dodie knew well was going to kill her, they've had lots of opportunities before now. The timing makes it more likely that someone like Korine, who has a more immediate reason, got rid of her."

Chaz had propped his feet up on the blond wood of the coffee table in front of him, his plate nestled in his lap. He objected, "There is no way that Mother could have put that woman in the bin."

"Your mom's a lot stronger than she looks," J.J. said, lifting a forkful of lo mein into his mouth. "She slings fifty-pound sacks of fertilizer around all the time. Dodie wasn't that big. And if they don't think about Korine's weight-lifting activities with respect to her work, then they're probably thinking that she had you—or me—or Leo—to help her hide the body.

Korine choked on her fried rice. "It's bad enough that they're treating this like a parlor game," she said to Janey. "Does J.J. have to come up with so many logical and compelling reasons for them to suspect me?"

A knock at the door made Korine jump. Chaz threw her a reassuring look and said, "That's probably Richard. He's later than I thought he would be. His court case must have gone over."

Chaz went out into the entryway to the suite and opened the door. A deep voice with the unmistakable drawl of Savannah answered his greeting. The two men spoke quietly for a moment before entering the room.

"Sorry," Chaz said. "I had to catch Richard up on what Mom and I have been through today."

They all stood, and introductions were given all around. Korine remembered Richard from Chaz's law school days, when the boys had roomed together one year. She'd never met Leslie, but she assumed the girl was as pretty as Richard was handsome. Whenever Chaz mentioned them, he spoke of the pair with fondness. Korine felt a brief twinge of anger, quickly suppressed, that Richard had found someone new.

Richard's eyes, dark brown like bitter chocolate, under thick brows, gave him a stern air, which Korine supposed stood him well in court. Personally, she found them a bit too probing, as if he were seeking her inmost soul rather than her assurance that she hadn't killed Dodie.

They sat. Korine took him through the events of the weekend, and he asked her to repeat the business with the microphone and the stain on the table earlier that morning.

"Very interesting," he pronounced. "And you're sure it wasn't blood?"

"I don't think so. I washed the blouse and hung it up in the bathroom."

"Which the police have cordoned off." Richard stared down at the pad upon which he'd written her story, tapping his Montblanc pen against his pursed lips. "Time to make a phone call or two." He picked up the phone, pressed nine, then a series of numbers that turned out to be the police station. He asked for Sudley's office.

When the phone was answered, Richard rattled off a list of information he needed. Korine didn't hear what he said, but his tone was sharp. He hung up and said, "Now we wait for those faxes to come in and we'll see what we see."

J.J. looked at his watch and said, "You'll be lucky if

they get around to sending you that stuff hours from now. Korine, I think we'll go on down and get out of your way so you can get some rest."

Janey gave Korine a hug and asked, "Do you want me to bring you some breakfast in the morning?"

"Thanks, but no," she said, thinking it over. "I don't know if I'll attend any of the conference proceedings, but being a prisoner in this room doesn't appeal to me. Maybe we could meet about eight and go out for something?"

"Don't worry. I'm sure Sharon will have realized by morning you can't have had anything to do with Dodie's death. It'll be fine for you to attend the last day of the conference," Janey said.

Korine nodded, even though she knew that, for her, the conference was over.

Walking over to the doorway, Janey and J.J. let themselves out while Richard, Chaz, and Korine put the last of the dinner leavings in the trash.

Facing the pair of men, Korine announced her intention to try and get some sleep. Richard looked at Chaz. At his nod, Richard said, "I think if it's all right with you, I'd like to ask you a few questions about Dodie and your relationship with her."

"Can it wait for morning?" Korine's voice emerged tired and weak, just like she felt.

The two men exchanged another look, using some kind of lawyerly extrasensory perception to make a decision.

Chaz hugged his mother. "We'll talk in the morning. Richard and I will meet you here about seven." He smiled slightly at Korine's protest about the early time.

"Believe me, Sudley will be on the job early in the morning, and you need to be ready for him."

Korine once again claimed the chenille chair by the window for her own.

"Do you want me to stay here tonight?" Chaz offered.

"No, go on home," she said. "I'll see you in the morning."

Chaz's blue eyes locked with Korine's. "You don't look so good. Are you sure you're all right to be alone?" he asked, kneeling in front of her.

"I'll be fine. What I need is a good night's rest."

Chaz shook his head slightly, his expression much closer to the normal exasperation he usually exhibited with her whenever she disagreed with him. Shrugging off any responsibility for her decision, he rose and followed Richard. Just before the door closed behind the two men, Korine heard them begin to argue.

She closed her eyes and held her shaking hands motionless in her lap. When she'd conquered her tremors, Korine pushed herself up and walked over to the phone on the counter of the bar. She picked it up, putting the cold plastic next to her ear. Even just dialing Amilou's number back home soothed Korine.

"Hello?" Amilou's voice came over the wire.

"It's Korine."

"What's wrong?" Just that fast Amilou had pinpointed trouble in Korine's voice. It was reassuring that, even this far away, calling a friend was the right thing to do.

"You remember how you told me what an unpleasant woman Dodie Halloran was, and how miserable I'd be if I went ahead and roomed with her?"

"Yes," Amilou said smugly, "in fact, I do. How are you two getting along?"

"Somebody murdered Dodie."

Amilou laughed uncertainly on the other end of the phone. "You are joking, aren't you?"

"I kid you not. They think I did it."

"Is J.J. there to tell them you didn't?"

"It doesn't matter. There's this man—"

"Dodie's man?"

"She evidently thought so. Anyway, he seems to think I might be more to his taste for this weekend."

"Who is it?" Amilou asked sharply.

"Leo Gilcrest. And worse, he feels so familiar," Korine said.

"Feels?" Amilou laughed uncertainly. *"Feels?"* she repeated, this time sounding incredulous. "So they think you killed Dodie over Leo Gilcrest?"

"Yes," Korine said, ignoring the dangerous choice of words she'd inadvertently used to describe that odd feeling she had about Leo. "That and the business rivalry. I can't convince the policeman that neither one of those things would cause me to need to kill Dodie."

"I'll mail him out a profit-and-loss sheet for last year, and he can compare that to Dodie's. That will take care of the one. Now tell me about this man who's woken you from your grieving-widow role."

Korine gritted her teeth and began to wish she hadn't called Amilou. Her friend had never understood Korine's need to mourn Charlie's memory, or why it still seemed fresh seven years after the fact.

"I don't want to have anything to do with Leo Gilcrest!" The intensity of Korine's outburst silenced Amilou.

After the pause, in which Korine could almost see Amilou counting to ten to keep from yelling back, Amilou said, "Well. That's a rather strong reaction. Either you're finally figuring out that you didn't die when Charlie did, or something else is going on with Leo to make you back off that hard from him. Do you think he killed Dodie?"

"He might have." Korine could hear the anguish in her own voice. Why she ever thought that calling Amilou would be productive, she didn't know.

Amilou picked her words carefully. "Talk to J.J. I'd come down there if I could, but Arnold isn't letting me off the hook one little bit. I can't leave the Pine Grove city limits even to go to Dunville's for seed."

"I know." Korine felt bone weary. She looked through the door into the garish bedroom and knew that the night ahead would be a long one.

"Listen," Amilou said. "Just because this guy likes you, it doesn't make him an ax murderer. You're just out of practice at judging that. Stay away from him until you ask Janey and J.J. They're pretty good judges of character. Look how quick they had me pegged."

Korine managed a halfhearted laugh. "All right," she said, "I'll keep you informed." She knew better than to keep protesting about Leo. Amilou would just become more and more convinced that Korine wanted him. Perhaps that was the problem with Detective Sudley.

"Good," Amilou said. "I'll talk to you sometime tomorrow."

As Korine was about to put down the phone, Amilou added, "How's Chaz? He helping you out down there?"

Briefly, Korine related Chaz's conversation that morning—or the lack thereof.

"Talk to him tomorrow," Amilou recommended. "At least you've got yourself two good lawyers. Now go to bed."

"Good night." Korine laid the phone to rest and walked into the bedroom. Grimacing, she prepared for bed.

Much later, as she lay tangled in the satin sheets on the blood-red bed, she gazed into the mirror on the ceiling. It reflected her own troubled eyes, huge in a pale face. Unable to even face herself, Korine rolled over and buried her face in the soft downy pillow.

She knew that wishing ill upon someone didn't actually make it happen. But if it could, she was as guilty as anyone in Dodie's death.

SEVEN

J.J. GOT UP EARLY THE next morning. Not as early as Janey, who had gotten up at her customary hour of six to undertake what she calls her "Sanity Journey." She walked two miles, every day, without fail. J.J. had told her how to find the coffee shop where he'd been the day before. He hoped she would stop there and bring him something for breakfast.

As he strapped his watch onto his wrist, he realized that Janey wasn't going to return before he was ready to go out. She must have gone up to Korine's room to talk. He would walk around the corner himself. After breakfast, he would see if he could find anyone to talk to about Dodie's death.

Exiting the elevator in the lobby, J.J. discovered that Janey wasn't up talking to Korine after all. He spotted his wife sipping a cup of coffee in the hotel restaurant, and he watched her for a moment from behind a post. She and a young woman, long dark hair swinging in time to her animated conversation, had their heads bowed together. Janey was talking to Holly Winslow.

He wanted to go in and shake Janey for interfering. He knew that it was counterproductive to let suspects know that they were under investigation. Since he wasn't an official on this case, he settled for waving at the pair as he passed by the doors. He'd talk with Janey later, in private, and make it clear that he meant it when he told her to stay out of things.

Deciding to postpone breakfast until he could find some information to chew on to go with the sweet rolls or jelly doughnuts, J.J. headed down the escalator to the conference level. A group of men discussing how best to spread dirt rode down behind him. At the bottom, he looked around and saw no one of interest. Perhaps, if he got lucky, he'd run into Sudley and be able to convince the detective to give him a look at the scene of the crime.

J.J. entered the service corridor. It was deserted. No policemen. No linen carts containing dead bodies. There was, however, a mark on the floor from the day before, showing where the cart in question had stood. It wasn't three paces from the crime-scene-marked door to the conference room where Dodie had supposedly been killed.

Janey had said that Leo Gilcrest entered the room through those service doors shortly after Korine heard Dodie's argument over the PA. If J.J. was going to make the same mistake that Sudley had, and decide who had killed Dodie before he looked at any clear evidence, he'd pick Leo Gilcrest. Yes, it was highly interesting timing. But J.J. still reserved final judgment. He couldn't figure out the whys of the timing of Dodie's death. It had to have something to do with the combination of people involved in this weekend's conference.

The temptation to open the door and step into the crime scene itself was overwhelming. J.J. was able to resist only because he knew how angry he would be if someone interfered with one of his own investigations. Everything he had done up to that point could not be construed as meddling. Or so he told himself.

Reluctantly, he turned away and started to exit the hallway. Voices outside the door stopped him. Leo's deep voice, playing counterpoint to Sharon's whiny soprano, filtered through the crack in the doors. Since eavesdropping came under the list of non-meddling activities, J.J. eased his ear over toward the opening.

"How dare you suggest that!" He could almost see Sharon's indignation through the wood.

"You're outright accusing me of the same thing," Leo said. In contrast, Leo's voice was calm, low, and even. Very cool, when faced with an angry woman.

"You played Dodie along for years. First you asked her to marry you, then you walked out on her the day before your wedding."

"I'm not proud of that," Leo replied. "But, perhaps more important than your feelings on that matter, was the fact that Dodie had forgiven me, even if I hadn't forgiven myself. I know she wanted me to fall in love with her again, but it just wasn't possible. Not after what she did."

J.J. had pushed the door open enough so that he could see a sliver of this action. Sharon's profile showed. Leo must be directly behind the door. Even with the limited view, he could see Leo's words hit Sharon and rock her back.

"What she did?" Sharon's voice was faint. J.J. more read her white lips than heard her.

"You know what I'm talking about."

"No!" Sharon's low cry sounded like a lost soul going down for the last time. "You can't be—"

"I am perfectly serious. You have to know. She confided everything in you." Leo's voice was tired as dust. "She stole the one thing I wanted more than anything else in the world. I could understand what she did, but I could never forgive her."

"I thought—" Sharon stopped and bit her lip. "What about Korine?"

"She knows nothing about this, and she never will, you hear me?" As Leo took a step closer to Sharon, his raised fist came into view. "I've loved that woman for close to forty years."

J.J. almost fell through the doorway in his surprise. Korine had never mentioned that she knew Leo Gilcrest from before! He felt a slow anger burn away at his confidence. What else had she kept from them?

Stuffing his personal feelings back into their mental lockbox, he caught Leo's next words: "I lost her once, but I'll be damned if I lose her again. Korine Stewart is the person I'm meant to be with."

"Why didn't you go find Korine when your wife died, rather than leading Dodie on instead?" Sharon asked.

In the intensity of their discussion, both voices had dropped to whisper level. J.J. moved slightly so that he could hear better.

"Korine was married and had a child," Leo replied. His hand dropped to his side, anger forgotten. Every line of his body spoke of the effort it had taken to let Korine go. "The time wasn't right. I turned to Dodie, and you know how that went."

"Dodie moved up to the mountains," Sharon began.

"To be near Korine to find out more about her," Leo finished. "Don't I know it," he said bitterly. He moved backward, bumping the door that J.J. held open.

J.J. let go of the door and sprinted down the hallway, ducking through the door at the opposite end. Standing there, panting for a moment, he was pretty sure that Leo hadn't noticed the door had been open when he hit it.

It was something to think on, Dodie's plan when she moved. Was she after information? Or revenge? The fact that she'd gone into the landscaping business in direct competition with Korine, Janey, and Amilou's company was telling.

It would also be necessary, and tricky, to find out what Dodie had done that had caused Leo to break off their engagement the day before their wedding. How long had Dodie nursed this anger? Blaming a forty-year-old romance was a bit much. Sharon had asked why Leo hadn't gone to Korine after his wife died. It was certainly more than seven years ago. If Leo loved Korine that intensely, why hadn't he come forward immediately when Charlie died?

Walking in what he sincerely hoped was an offhand manner, he found Leo and Sharon partially screened from view by the ever-present potted palms, secluded in the corner by the service doors. The scant number of conference-goers in the hallway gave the pair a wide berth. Inhaling slowly, J.J. headed in their direction. As he came up on them, Sharon stood with her back to him.

"I didn't kill Dodie!" she said. "Why would I do that? You know how much I owe her. Besides, you're—" Sharon turned around, following Leo's gaze as it transferred from her face to the point behind her shoulder which contained J.J.'s own sweet self. She took one look at J.J., burst into tears, and walked rapidly away.

With regret, he stood there and watched her go. He'd have to try and catch up with her later. J.J. wished he'd stayed in place behind the doors. He would have liked to have heard exactly what it was that Dodie had done for Sharon. Not to mention what Leo Gilcrest's role had been. He let that regret go. If they had discovered him hiding there, he'd never get anywhere with them later.

"I'm sorry," he apologized to Leo. "I didn't mean to interrupt."

Leo gave him a hard stare. "You're the police chief in Pine Grove. How do you go about finding out who killed someone?"

J.J. wondered how Leo knew his profession. Had he been watching Korine that closely, or had he talked to Janey? "I usually talk to everyone involved. Get the lab to check on a bunch of stuff. Spend lots of time on the phone."

"Can you find out who killed Dodie?"

"The Savannah police are perfectly capable of solving this without me or you," J.J. said.

"I'm not so sure. It matters to me that they catch whoever did this to Dodie."

"I thought you didn't like her."

"Not liking Dodie and wanting her dead are two separate ticket items," Leo returned. "I almost married that woman a long time ago. I'd like to know who did this to her."

"You and Dodie were married?" J.J. was pleased to hear that his voice sounded properly incredulous.

"*Not* married, which is why Sharon is all aflutter about my not paying enough attention to Dodie this weekend. She'd thought this conference would get us back together after all these years."

"How recently did you break up?" J.J. thought he sounded properly skeptical. Lay it on too thick, and Leo would either see through him or, perhaps worse, think J.J. was a doofus.

"Many years ago. Before I met Fiona," Leo said. "My wife," he added in response to J.J.'s questioning look. "I guess Dodie thought enough time had passed so that she could try and get me back." Leo lapsed into silence. Shoving his hands in his pockets, he jingled his keys for half a second, then met J.J.'s eyes. "Do you have a minute? I'd like to talk this out with someone who might understand."

The two men took the escalator up to the main level. Leo attracted several curious glances from people in the lobby. J.J. suggested the coffee shop around the corner as a way to avoid the crowd.

As they were leaving the hotel, J.J. saw Korine step

off the elevator. Leo saw her too, and his whole body went on point.

"Do you want to tell me about Dodie, or do you want to tell me about you and Korine?" J.J. asked.

Leo swung his head around and stared at J.J. "Noticing sort of guy, aren't you?"

"It's the policeman in me. I didn't choose the job, it chose me."

Leo gave him an inquiring stare, but J.J. didn't elaborate. It wasn't his past that bore examination here. The two men walked in silence to the coffee shop.

J.J. held the glass door open for Leo and then followed him inside. Each of them got a glass of tea and settled into the vinyl-seated booth in the corner. A girl with pink hair and a nose ring bigger than a bull's walked by the window. She couldn't have been more than twelve.

J.J. settled back in his seat. If not for the purple and green decor and the girl outside the window, he could have been in the Green Whistle Café back home. Feeling more like he was on familiar ground, he glued his eyes to Leo's face and waited.

Leo drained half his glass in one sip, Adam's apple bobbing rapidly as the cool liquid disappeared. Setting the glass on the table, he met J.J.'s gaze squarely. "I suppose you're wondering what that was all about back there."

J.J. nodded and waited.

"I had to ask Sharon some hard questions. She's been acting kind of strange all through this weekend. First, she and Dodie would have a fight, then Sharon would pick on somebody else and say it was because of something Dodie had told her."

"I'd noticed that," J.J. said dryly. The outburst in the lobby that first night stuck in his mind.

"Then yesterday morning, Sharon was working on setting up that Tropical Room with all those native plants she'd gotten together. She ripped her shirt and went out to change it. Only, she went down, not up to her room when she got on the elevator."

"Maybe she just didn't notice."

"Sharon noticed all right. She'd missed one up-elevator, pretending to talk with the hotel liaison. I'm thinking that she went down and killed Dodie."

"What time did you see Sharon leave the Tropicana Room?"

"Tropical Room," Leo corrected absently. "It might have been around eight-thirty."

"You do realize that you walked right past Dodie's body in that service hall when you met Korine and Janey in the conference room?"

Leo closed his eyes and massaged one eyebrow with shaking fingers. "No, I didn't know that. Thanks for sharing it with me, though. It's the perfect irony to top an already horrid day. I was looking for Dodie when I poked my head in and found Korine and your wife. I'd been in the lobby until a few minutes before, talking with Holly. She told me she thought she'd seen Dodie go into that room earlier."

J.J.'s stomach rumbled. He gestured to the waitress,

and she came over and took his order for breakfast. Leo declined, his face still drawn and tinged with green.

"I hope she didn't suffer," Leo said.

"Oh, Dodie suffered," J.J. answered. "But the killer cared enough about her to tidy her up a bit, so she wasn't all thrown-away looking when she was found. In my mind, that leans the suspicion more toward someone who was related to her in some way."

Leo gave J.J. a sharp look. "Like Sharon."

"Or you. Or Holly. Or even Holly's father, who I haven't seen yet."

Leo's expression acknowledged the hit. J.J. waited to see if the man would respond to his suggestion that he had killed his former fiancée.

"George Winslow," Leo said, "wouldn't get within a hundred yards of Dodie if he could help it. She vamped him a bit when he and Sharon got married, and he's never felt comfortable with her since. He sure wouldn't have—how did you put it?—tidied her up."

"And what about Korine? As her friend, I'm wondering what your intentions are toward her."

"How old-fashioned. You and Mrs. Stewart, Korine's mother, must get along well." Leo's voice held an edge that had previously been missing.

"How long have you and Korine known each other?"

"We knew each other a long time ago. I don't want to discuss it with you until I've had a chance to talk more with Korine. Dodie's death has changed everything I'd planned for this weekend."

J.J. felt his eyebrows raise in response to Leo's

statement. They rose even farther with Leo's next request.

His hand shaking, Leo drew a hundred-dollar bill out of his tooled-leather wallet and laid it on the table. Placing his hand on it, he pushed it over to J.J. "I want you to find out how Sharon Winslow killed Dodie. I want that woman punished for what she's done."

EIGHT

KORINE WOKE FROM a vivid and disturbing dream about Dodie. She thrust the memory of it from her, only to be filled with misgivings of another sort. Lying there in the tangle of satin sheets, head buried in the pillow, she couldn't escape that air of familiarity surrounding Leo Gilcrest. She didn't know him, did she? The hell of it was that whether she knew him, or just thought she did, she still found him attractive.

Dragging herself to her feet, Korine threw the covers back on the bed behind her and headed to the bathroom. She unzipped the plastic vanity kit—inexplicably the only item the police had returned to her the day before—and plunged her hand deep inside. Fumbling around, she came to the unwelcome conclusion that her toothbrush and toothpaste were missing.

She glanced down at the large T-shirt Chaz had loaned her the night before so that she wouldn't have to sleep in her clothes. Phoning room service, Korine asked them to bring up a spare toothbrush and toothpaste. She crossed over to the large closet and pulled open the door. Hanging there, lonely and abandoned looking, were her clothes from the day before. She slipped them off the hanger and began to dress. It wouldn't do to answer the door wearing only Chaz's iguana-print T-shirt.

While Korine waited, she went out and made a pot of coffee. As it brewed, she went over and drew back the curtain so that she could look out. A light rotated lethargically on top of a building down by the river. She had plenty of time to prepare herself before Richard and Chaz came to talk with her. It was, after all, only five o'clock in the morning.

Fifteen minutes later, a knock came at the door and Korine abandoned her post by the window. She fumbled with her purse and came up with a few wrinkled dollars to tip the young man. Shutting the door behind her, Korine went back into the bathroom to brush her teeth with what was surely the most expensive toothbrush in North America.

It worked too. The combination of scrubbing and minty taste brought more energy to her brain than the coffee had earlier. It lasted her until she went to open the door for her son. The serious expressions on his and Richard's faces, however, sapped the energy right out of her.

"Come on in." Korine swung the door open wide for the two men, then followed them into the room.

"Sleep well?" Chaz asked as he bussed Korine's cheek.

"Not really." She threw a glance at the closed door of her bedroom. They settled into the chairs.

Richard snapped open the locks on his leather briefcase. Pulling out a small stack of papers, he began asking questions. "How long have you known Dodie Halloran?"

"I told you that," Korine said impatiently. "What did

they send over?" She craned her neck trying to see around the corner of the paper that Richard held in his hand.

He looked up at her from over the rim of a pair of reading glasses. "Just answer the question, Korine. Sudley won't let you get away with this, you know."

"I met her two days ago when I checked into the hotel. I knew her only by reputation before that."

"So if you knew her by reputation—and didn't care much for that, if your tone of voice is anything to judge by—why did you room with her?"

"Sharon made those arrangements. I didn't know until I got here who my roommate would be."

Richard handed the paper over to Korine and looked back over his shoulder at Chaz. Shaking his head slightly, her son walked over to the window and stared out at the sleepy city.

Korine looked down. Autopsy results. She shuddered, then handed the sheet back again. "Can you tell me the pertinent parts?" she asked.

"Oleander, just like the stain found on your shirt and Leo Gilcrest's pants."

Korine felt faint. "So they think I did it, don't they?"

"We should have done this last night. No way you'll be ready for Sudley this morning." Richard got up abruptly and went over to Chaz. Though Richard spoke softly, Korine could still hear him say, "We've got to get somebody else for her. I'm going to wind up compromising the case because I know the two of you."

She stood up and walked over to him. "I don't want someone else. You're Chaz's friend, and that's enough for me. Besides, you said yourself that you have a good working relationship with Detective Sudley."

Richard looked at her again over the top of his glasses. Coldly assessing her, he finally nodded his head. "Let's work on some other things," he said as they took their seats once more. "You don't seem to realize how serious this all is. Sudley has one of the best arrest records in Savannah's history. I can't help you beyond a certain point. As it is, this may be judged as a conflict of interest."

"Why?"

"Because I work in the office that would prosecute you if Sudley digs up enough evidence to arrest you."

Korine sat still and then drew a breath before replying. "If you're willing to jeopardize your job, then I'll do whatever you say I need to do."

Richard took off his glasses and rubbed his eyes. Still massaging them, he asked, "Why do you think that Sharon put you in with Dodie?"

"I don't know." At Richard's look of disbelief, Korine added, "Really. I have no idea why she'd do something like that. Unless…." She paused. "Unless, Dodie had asked her to."

"And why would Dodie do something like that?"

"To get me to help her out with her business," Korine replied. "I can't imagine any other reason—although, from the minute I walked through the door, she seemed as if she didn't even like me. I think it pained her as much as it did me that we were in the same room."

"So that's something we'll have to ask Sharon." Richard made a note.

Chaz moved away from the window. "Mother, did Dodie's dislike have anything to do with Leo Gilcrest?"

Korine thought carefully before answering. "It could have; they certainly have a history together. But I don't know why she'd be angry with me from the get-go. I hadn't even met Leo yet." Her voice wavered as she remembered her dream and the feeling she'd had upon awakening. She *had* met Leo before, but for the life of her, she couldn't remember where.

"What?" Richard's voice was knife sharp.

"Nothing," Korine said, but even she could tell that her voice was unconvincing.

"Mother!" Chaz exclaimed. "What is it?"

"He seems familiar, but I swear I don't think I've ever met him before. I can't explain it."

Richard rose and looked at his watch. "You'd better either learn to hide it more effectively, figure out where it is that you know him from, or come up with a better explanation for Sudley when he arrives." He snapped shut the locks on his case and picked it up. "I'm going over to the police station to pick up some more information—if they'll give it to me. I had to fight to get the autopsy report."

Korine looked at him, frightened by the serious look in his eyes.

He continued, "I got the impression from Sudley yesterday that you are one of several possibilities, but not the strongest. Don't give him reason to look even more closely at you."

"You think I killed her, don't you?"

Chaz made a negative sound as Richard responded. "No, I don't. But what I think doesn't matter when the case comes to trial."

As Richard walked toward the door, Chaz paused by his mother's chair. Covering her hand with his, he leaned down and looked directly into her eyes. "Just tell the truth, the whole truth, and nothing but the truth, and you'll be fine." He stood.

"You're leaving too?"

Chaz looked away, after his friend's retreating back. "Yes, I'll be more help to you this way. Just don't talk to Sudley until Richard or I get back." He handed her a card with a phone number scrawled on the back. "This is Richard's cell phone. Don't hesitate to call as soon as you need him back." The door closing behind him sounded final, as if she were being walled off from the world.

Korine stood up and went in to brush her hair. She hadn't done anything wrong. She was not about to sit in her room and wait for Sudley to find her cowering there. Arriving in the bathroom, Korine stuck her tongue out at herself in the mirror. She turned on the tap and reached for the washrag. Scrubbing her face, she began getting ready to go out.

CHECKING HER WATCH as she climbed on the elevator, Korine assumed that she'd missed meeting Janey for breakfast. There hadn't been an answer in her room, and it was already nine-thirty, an hour and a half past the time they'd planned on meeting.

Korine poked her head in the doorway of the restaurant, scanning the crowded tables. She spotted Janey, sitting at a table with Holly and Chaz. Over Holly's head, Korine and Janey made eye contact. Tapping one finger on her purse, Korine wondered why Chaz had abandoned her in her room to accompany Richard and then wound up here with Holly and Janey.

Chaz swiveled around. Beckoning her over to the table, he turned and said something to Holly. The girl frowned in response.

As Korine came into the restaurant, an eddy of quiet grew from the doorway until it enveloped the entire room. In the silence, a water glass hit the floor with a crash as one woman turned to look at Korine, who had frozen in front of the cash register. The noise broke the vocal paralysis, and a rash of conversation swelled around them.

Korine forced herself to enter the room. "Good morning," she said when she reached the table. If she didn't know that Janey was the most phlegmatic person on the face of the earth, she would have sworn that her friend was angry about something. Korine hoped she wasn't angry with her.

Fortunately for Holly, she took after her father rather than her mother. Pretty thing: slender, dark, and graceful. Pretty manners too, which, so far, Korine hadn't seen Sharon exhibit. Come to think of it, Holly's manners were better than her own. Korine was still standing awkwardly by the table, twisting her purse strap all out of shape. Emily Post didn't exactly have a page on what etiquette demanded when you came face to face with the cousin of the woman you had been accused of killing.

"Holly wanted someone to talk with," Janey said, correctly interpreting Korine's hesitation, "and I was here. She realizes—of course—that you had nothing to do with Dodie's death."

Korine threw her a glance of gratitude, before turning back to Chaz. "I thought you'd gone with Richard," she said. A note of self-pity had crept into her voice. She mentally banished it.

Janey pushed out the chair next to her. "We've finished, but we'll call the waiter back if you'd like."

Korine sat. Under cover of looking at the menu, she watched Chaz flirting with Sharon's daughter. When the waitress came, she ordered the country omelet special. She hated sausage in her eggs, but it was the only thing on the menu she could remember. Here she was, condemned by an entire room full of people who didn't even know her, and Chaz was finally interested in a woman—the cousin of a woman his mother might have killed, and the daughter of a woman who wanted to see Korine convicted of the crime.

She looked sideways at Janey and realized that her friend wasn't angry. A better word to describe the look Korine saw in Janey's eyes was preoccupation. She wondered what it was that had happened to upset Janey. Irrationally, she wished that Janey would calm down and pay attention to the fact that Korine was close to panic.

Far from noticing Korine's dilemma, Janey rose. "I'd better get going. I saw J.J. go out a while back, and he wanted to do some things with me today. I'd better go find the man and see what it was that he wanted."

She walked out of the restaurant, leaving behind a very nervous Korine. Chaz didn't look like he was going anywhere. Korine thought she'd like a Bloody Mary, but she decided against it. Who knows what people would have said.

"More coffee?" Chaz asked solicitously—of Holly, not his mother. At her affirmative, he took Holly's cup and went over to the buffet table and filled it. While he was picking up packets of sugar and creamer to replenish the empty glass container at their table, Korine asked Holly which sessions she was going to attend.

"I couldn't possibly enjoy anything today! Dodie was like a second mother to me." Holly sounded as if she would break into tears at any moment.

This abrupt departure from the mannerly greeting stiffened Korine's smile, and she struggled to stop dismay from distorting her features. Was this how Amilou had felt while the whole town watched to see if she'd killed her own husband? Korine had gotten a taste of the feeling when she walked into the room, but people seemed to have gotten over it, making conversation just like normal.

Holly's reaction brought home to Korine just how people would respond to her as the day progressed. It was almost enough to send her fleeing back upstairs to that padded cage of a room. She had known that she wouldn't enjoy the rest of the weekend as she'd planned.

What she hadn't known was how very dismal her chances were of enjoying anything at all.

Chaz took one look at both their faces when he returned and said, "Leave you alone for one minute...." He kicked out the chair and sat down, drawing it back under him gracefully. "Listen to me," he said, looking from his mother to the doe-eyed young woman and back again. "People will talk. They will say things that neither one of you wants to hear."

He leaned toward Holly. "People are going to say that they never speak ill of the dead, then they'll tell you in great detail why they never liked Dodie."

Turning to Korine, Chaz said, "People are going to avoid you. They might like you fine, but it's an odd feeling, knowing that the person sitting next to them might be a killer."

He looked back at Holly. "Actually, they're going to look at your whole family that way too." He ignored Holly's indignant gasp. Cutting off Korine's similar protest with a stern look, he said, "It's nothing personal. It's just one of those things. It doesn't matter who actually did it; both of you are targets for people's curiosity right now. Be prepared."

Korine gathered her purse from under the table. "I suppose you're right," she said heavily. "But do we have to treat each other that way?"

Chaz looked from his mother to Holly and back again.

"You're right," Holly said abruptly. "I don't know who killed Dodie, but whoever it was, we owe it to each other to act civilly until they figure out who did it."

Korine didn't appreciate being the object of Chaz's lecture—not even if he was in the right of it. She sat, ramrod stiff while she debated what to do.

Holly and Chaz exchanged a look that people of a younger generation had been exchanging for eternity. Korine was getting very tired of watching the nonverbal communication of other people.

She stood; she wasn't up to this right now. "Thanks for breakfast. Chaz, you'll take care of the check for me, won't you? It seems I need to figure out how to make myself scarce today."

Blindly, Korine fled the restaurant. She knew that the two of them—or the whole room, for all she knew—were staring at her back, but she couldn't seem to slow down. Punching the button viciously, she cursed the hotel designers for installing the main bank of elevators in full view of the restaurant.

The doors opened and she dove inside. As soon as they closed she knew that she'd traded one problem for another. Detective Sudley stood in the corner, watching her.

NINE

BEFORE KORINE COULD even think, Sudley reached out and punched the button for her floor. "Just the woman I was looking for," he said. "Do you mind if we talk in your room?"

Korine was beginning to hate rhetorical questions. "If the alternative is in the lobby or in your office, then yes, that would be fine," she answered.

Sudley looked steadily back at Korine, the pained expression in his storm-gray eyes making her feel guilty for having been snippy. As the elevator got closer to her floor, Korine irrationally wished Richard hadn't felt the need to rush to the police station that morning. He might have been more useful staying at the hotel. Korine took her frustration out on her purse, pulling the bag more tightly up her shoulder. With dismay, she heard the strap give.

The bag hit the hard floor of the elevator with a crash. Lipstick and paper flew everywhere. Sudley and Korine knelt on the floor to retrieve lost pencils, seeds, and coins. Korine accepted a French jetton from Sudley's outstretched hand. She'd meant to clean out her purse before coming on this trip but somehow had never gotten around to it. She'd had that jetton in her purse for at least three years, since Chaz had come back from a trip to Paris and given it to her.

As the doors opened, Sudley scrambled to his feet, sticking his hand on the door to hold it open. Korine put one hand on the metal door casing to support herself as she stood. Her palm slipped on the slick polished chrome. Losing her balance, she threw her other hand out to catch herself before she fell flat on her face. The torn seed packet she was holding fluttered out of her hand, slipping down into the crack between the elevator and the hallway.

"We'll get it for you later," Sudley said, putting his hand beneath her elbow to steady her.

Korine looked up at him, disconcerted by the warmth of his hand on her arm. "They're just free seeds from a table in the exhibitor's hall. Don't worry about it."

He smiled, the wrinkles around his eyes crinkling as he said, "I'm not a bit worried."

The detective stood to the side to allow her to exit the elevator. Korine felt her back setting up as she passed him. This was the second man to invade her personal space in two days. At least Leo had been honest about his motives. With Sudley, that physical crowding was just a trick to throw her off. Her dislike of the officer deepened.

They arrived at her room. Just outside the door stood an uncertain bellhop, holding her old, battered navy Samsonite suitcase in one hand. Korine fumbled in her purse and came up with a few dollars with which to tip the poor boy. Gratefully, she took the case and unlocked the door to the suite.

Walking into the bedroom, she crossed the expanse of pink fluffy carpet and tossed the case on the bed. Sudley followed her into the room and whistled. Korine hadn't slept at all after waking up from her dream, and the sheets were twisted every which way.

"Do you mind?" she asked.

"No, go right ahead," Sudley answered. The heartless man knew exactly what she'd been asking, yet he didn't have the decency to leave her alone.

She flipped open the latches on the suitcase and opened it. Inside was a bundle of fluff. Korine frowned. It wasn't hers. She held up a frothy negligee. Turning to Sudley, she handed the confection toward him. "Your men were a little overzealous in packing," she said primly. She let the thing fall into his outstretched hand. "This must have been Dodie's. I thought you said that Sharon had gone through and identified Dodie's things." Her eyes narrowed.

Sudley looked amused. "This was in a box on your bed," he said. "Sharon assumed it was yours."

"Sharon assumed wrong." Korine snapped shut the latches and swung around, intending to walk past Sudley into the other room and call Richard on his cell phone, refusing to say another word to the officer until her lawyer arrived.

Sudley slung the pale pink swatch of lace and chiffon over his shoulder. One eyebrow hitched up as he looked down at Korine.

She struggled with the inappropriate urge to giggle at the sight of the policeman festooned with Dodie's clothing. Evidently, the Good Cop had surfaced, and he was Sudley. Excusing herself incoherently from between clenched teeth, she pushed past the man and out into the main room. Throwing herself into the cozy armchair by the window, Korine struggled to keep from releasing the hysterical laughter that shook her. Plucking a tissue from the box on the table next to her, she settled for blowing her nose.

Sudley followed, having rid himself of the clinging fabric, and offered his assistance. Korine waved him off. "Oh, for goodness' sake, leave me be. I'm fine," she lied.

Korine could have sworn she saw a smile behind Sudley's dour mask as he turned and went over to use the phone. She was able to compose herself by the time he hung up.

The door to the hall slammed open, drowning Sudley's words of apology. "Mother?" Chaz came into the room, stopping short when he saw Sudley standing there. "What are you doing here?" Chaz asked the man.

"Your mother allowed as how she'd talk with me," Sudley responded. "We haven't started the interrogation yet. You're in plenty of time."

"I was just about to call Richard and see if he needed to be here when I talked with Detective Sudley," Korine reassured Chaz. She got up and poured a glass of water and handed it to her son, who still wore the pained look he'd acquired downstairs.

Chaz eyed her suspiciously, then took a cautious sip from the glass. "He hasn't tried to ask anything about you and Dodie?"

"No," she said. "A bellhop brought back my suitcase, and I opened it. It had something of Dodie's in it, which may be his way of questioning me, but I doubt it." Korine stopped to direct a sharp look at Sudley, who smothered a grin.

"He's a policeman, Mother. They get paid to be roundabout with their suspects."

"I'm beginning to see that," she said sharply, erasing the smile from Sudley's lips. Turning her back to the detective, Korine spoke to Chaz in a low voice. "I'm glad you're here. Now we can get down to business and get this questioning thing out of the way. You can advise me as well as Richard can." Somehow she had to convince Sudley that—however improbable people might find it with Dodie living in the next town over—Korine and Dodie had never met until that weekend.

Korine was just as happy to have Chaz as she would have been if Richard had been there. The more she'd thought about it, the more Richard's questions that morning had left her with the feeling that he considered her incompetent to handle questioning. Did he think that she was over the hill, or too unintelligent to remember how serious this all was? As if she could forget it.

"You don't like Richard?" Chaz asked, his worried eyes searching her face.

"I didn't say that." Korine wasn't about to tell her son that she out and out didn't like one of his nearest and dearest friends. "You said he was a good lawyer; I believe you. I also know that *you're* a good lawyer too. Look how well you did for Amilou."

Chaz swallowed the last of his water and waved her back over to the policeman's side with his empty glass. She sat, gratefully, in the club chair. Her hand once again stroked the soft nap of the fabric while Chaz and Sudley got themselves situated.

Sudley looked apologetic as he pulled the small tape recorder out of his pocket. He then flipped open the notebook that policemen don't seem to be able to leave their offices without. "Do you mind if I record this?" he asked.

Another one of those damn rhetorical questions. Maybe Chaz was right. Maybe all policemen—with the possible exception of J.J.—were devious and uninspired men who would just as soon put an innocent woman in jail as find the true killer. Still, Korine knew better than to say she minded. She nodded her assent.

Sudley made her say it out loud for the tape. After Korine put herself on record, the detective continued, "We went through quite a bit of this territory yesterday, but as I'm sure you're aware, when new information comes to light, we have to go back over old ground again with the people involved." He looked up from his paper scribbling to make certain that she was paying attention.

New information? Korine couldn't tear her eyes away from the man.

"How long have you known Leo Gilcrest?" Sudley asked.

"We went over this yesterday," Korine said, delaying the inevitable. "What new information?"

"Gilcrest?" Sudley prompted.

"I've known of Leo Gilcrest for years. He's quite well-known in gardening circles."

"Can you explain about why he would claim to have known you for thirty—no...." Sudley flipped back a few pages in his notebook. "Ah, here it is. Thirty-seven years?"

"No idea." Korine sat, holding herself still.

"Mr. Gilcrest said you might not remember. He said it had been a while since your paths had crossed." He flipped his notebook back to the current page and wrote something down.

Chaz stretched just right so that he could see what was on the page. Surprise dawned on his face. Sudley turned such a self-satisfied look on him that it confirmed Korine's earlier accusation about the detective's deviousness. He'd meant for Chaz to see whatever notes he had on that page.

"You went to high school with Gilcrest?" Chaz asked.

Not trusting her voice, Korine didn't respond.

"I believe he went by his step-daddy's name then," Sudley said. "McGilley."

Korine felt her nails curl into the fabric of the chair. Trust Mick—or Leo, as she now thought of him—to tell the police officer that they were involved without telling him the specifics. Lowrie High School, in the wilds of Tidewater, Virginia, was a long time ago. "Mick" McGilley had been a gangly boy who had chased her silly all during their junior year. He had disappeared over the summer before her senior year, never to be seen or heard from again. Korine hadn't recognized him because she didn't want to recognize him. The tragedy that resulted from their first—and last—date was burned indelibly into her memory. She wondered what else had changed about him, in addition to his name.

"I wonder why he didn't introduce himself to me with both names?" Korine said.

"Gilcrest said something about water under the bridge. Perhaps you could be more specific."

"We weren't friends. Different circles, you know," Korine said primly.

"I'm afraid I may have to insist."

Korine leveled a look at Sudley that would have had most people she knew writhing with discomfort. His face grew, if possible, even more amused. She said, "I don't know what he's talking about."

"He's obviously interested in your 'friendship' now."

"And, as I've repeatedly told you, I do not share his interest." Korine looked steadily back at him. She hoped he wasn't a mind reader. The conflicting feelings she held about Leo Gilcrest could have welded sheet metal. Sudley met her gaze, gray eyes serious. Nodding once, as if ticking something off a mental checklist, he bent his head and made a few marks on the page.

Chaz spoke up. "If you can't find something a little fresher to link Mother to this, then you don't need to be wasting your time here."

A brief look of anger crossed Sudley's face, leaving it hard and mean. Korine wanted to shake Chaz. It was bad enough that her son had played games with J.J. in his capacity as police chief of Pine Grove. He'd gotten away with it because J.J. knew him well enough to know when the games were harmless and when they masked a secret. Sudley didn't have that history. Pushing him was not a good idea.

"Can you go over for me what happened yesterday?" the detective asked. "Who you saw and when?"

At Chaz's resigned nod of assent, Korine started her story once again. Beginning with the pounding on the door of the bathroom and repeating that she didn't know with whom Dodie had been arguing either time, she included the information she'd forgotten to tell him the day before about turning off the microphone in the room where Dodie had apparently died.

That she'd forgotten anything at all brought a scowl to Sudley's face. She answered all the extra questions that he brought up, finishing her story without adding any more new information.

Finally, goaded beyond patience with his repeated questions about Leo Gilcrest's presence at Tybee Beach, she snapped. "No, I didn't make plans to meet him there. I don't know how many times I need to tell you before you believe me that I didn't know Leo and Mick were one and the same. If I had known, I would have made even more of an effort to avoid him."

Korine paused, near tears. She'd thought that Richard's questioning had been difficult. Perhaps he had been doing her a favor, preparing her for things to come.

Sudley snapped shut his notebook and turned off the tape recorder. "I think I'd better get back downstairs and check on a few things." He stood.

Korine and Chaz followed suit. They exchanged

glances that showed clearly they both agreed it was surprising that he would give up so abruptly.

"May I borrow your phone before I go?" Sudley was back to the Bad Cop persona he'd evinced the day before. The policeman's chameleon-like changes in the way he presented himself threw Korine. She couldn't get a firm feeling about him. Probably his intent.

"Certainly," she answered, indicating the phone on the table next to him.

Sudley's hand went to his waist and pulled a small pager off his belt. Glancing at it, he smiled tightly and picked up the phone. Dialing an in-house phone number, he slid the receiver between ear and shoulder and pulled the notebook out again. "Sudley here," he said.

"Uh-huh," he growled, scribbling frantically.

"Mmm. Really? Thanks." He replaced the phone on the hook, flipped the notebook shut, and turned to Korine. "I'll be back in touch with you. One of the men will retrieve your seed packet. We'll get it back to you as soon as we can."

"Why all this trouble? I told you they were just some free seeds I picked up at one of the vendors' booths. Zinnias, I think," Korine said.

"He's looking for the murder weapon," Chaz said to his mother. He turned to Sudley and said, "Aren't you?"

The detective looked steadily back at Chaz. "Of course. No reason to think it's Mrs. McFaile's seeds, but can't leave anything to chance, now can I? From what I saw before it fell, the contents weren't seeds. It was fine green powder."

Korine felt like a june bug right before the other shoe drops. All she could do was shake her head. If it was whatever had killed Dodie, she had no idea how it had gotten into her purse.

"I'll be in touch," Sudley said. "Don't go anywhere?"

Korine knew it wasn't really a question.

TEN

AS SOON AS THE DOOR SHUT behind Sudley, Chaz threw his pen across the room. It hit the wall by the bedroom door and bounced off onto the floor. Shoving himself out of the chair, he walked over and retrieved the pen.

"Do you want to tell Richard, or shall I?" Chaz didn't look at Korine as he asked his question.

She traced a path around the top of her water glass. "Mick—Leo—and I went out in high school, Chaz. As you so succinctly pointed out to the police: So?"

"So?" Chaz repeated sarcastically. "Leo-baby has obviously not forgotten." He stood twirling the pen around in his fingers.

The fact that he hadn't looked her directly in the eye since Sudley left wasn't lost on Korine. Her son was angry. And he didn't even know the half of it yet.

As if reading Korine's thoughts, Chaz turned and looked at her critically. "I don't know why," he said, "but I got the feeling Sudley doesn't think you killed Dodie."

"I didn't get that feeling at all," she countered.

"Where did you get those seeds?" Chaz asked.

"I picked up a few packets here and there. Zinnias, vegetables, that sort of thing. But not oleander. What would I be doing with that? It doesn't grow up in our area. Besides, I couldn't have poisoned her. I only ate with her Friday night. Although…," Korine said as she reviewed the repeated questions Sudley had thrown at her. "Maybe he was trying to get me to admit that Leo had a strong motive for murdering Dodie."

"Possibly." Chaz shoved the pen back into his pocket and sat down. Looking at her for the first time since Sudley left the room, his eyes were cool. Worry lines surrounded them. Even though she knew how old he was, the thought slipped in: *When had Chaz gotten old enough to have worry lines?*

He spoke. "I know you didn't do it. Who *did* know Dodie well enough to want to kill her?"

"Sharon Winslow," Korine said without hesitation.

"Motive?"

"Chronic irritation?"

Chaz gave that one the look it deserved.

"It's usually money, isn't it?" she said.

"Or love," Chaz reminded her, not very gently. He was stuck on the subject of Leo Gilcrest.

"Was Dodie ever married?" Korine asked, sitting up straight. "Any husband of hers would have a strong motive to kill her."

"You were the one rooming with the woman. Was she?"

"We didn't exactly stay up all night discussing our lives, Chaz. She yelled at me for hogging the bathroom, and she turned out my light on her way to bed so that I wouldn't disturb her. Then she snored all night. She didn't talk in her sleep—which would have been the only way I could have found out anything personal about her.

"The sad thing is," Korine continued, thinking back to the odd expression she'd glimpsed on Dodie's face before the woman fled into the shower the morning of her death, "I think she was afraid of people. That's why she acted the way she did."

"The sad thing," Chaz said, his voice uncompromising, "is that Dodie Halloran is dead and you're a suspect. Feeling sorry for her isn't going to figure out who killed her."

A knock at the door heralded Richard's return. As he preceded Chaz into the room, Korine was struck by the contrast in their coloring. Where Chaz was fair, as Charlie had been, with twinkling blue eyes, Richard had dark brown hair, flecked here and there with premature gray. His eyes were serious, brooding, and dark, dark brown, like water-smoothed stones in the New River back home. She'd not liked him the night before, and that dislike had solidified during the difficult morning question-and-answer session he'd subjected her to.

She had to admit it. Her initial dislike was based on Chaz's tale of the impending breakup between Richard and Leslie. Korine shook her head. Holding his personal life against him wasn't going to get her anywhere. And she had to admit that she was better prepared for Sudley's questions than she would have been without Richard's probing. She decided to revise her opinion of him. If he gave her good reason to do so.

"Did you get the information you needed?" she asked Richard.

"Yes, I think so." He took the chair next to hers. Clearing his throat, he glanced over at Chaz. Something passed between the two men that Korine couldn't identify. Lawyer ESP again, she supposed.

"You'd better go ahead and tell me," she said.

"They found something unusual on the blouse you'd sent down to the laundry."

"Unusual?" Korine revised her opinion of Richard's eyes. Lichen-covered stones. Soft, yet uncompromising in their honesty. There was a kernel of pity there. She swallowed. When Richard didn't continue, she made a gesture of frustration. "Well? Are you going to tell me what it was, or not?" she demanded.

"There was a poisonous substance, as yet unidentified, mixed in a tomato-juice base."

The disturbing memory of Leo Gilcrest leaning in, then brushing the stain off her blouse hit Korine. She reminded Richard of that, and the fact that Janey had witnessed how it got on Korine's blouse. "I'll bet it's oleander." Quickly, she summarized Sudley's news about the seed packet and the cause of Dodie's death.

Richard acknowledged that information soberly, then continued. "I'm not sure how we can effectively answer the seed-packet dilemma. However, you have a witness as to how the stain got on your shirt. Leo also has some explaining to do. Consistent with your story is the fact that his clothes were stained with the same substance that your blouse had on the sleeve."

Putting a hand up to forestall Korine's protest, Richard said, "I know you saw him brush up against the stain too, but what if that was deliberate?" He nodded as he saw Korine absorb that one.

"And I could have brushed against it just as deliberately."

"Exactly." Richard's eyes crinkled at the corners very slightly. He shot Chaz a glance that said, clearly, he approved of her.

Absurdly, Korine was pleased.

"Sudley's probably talking with Janey now," Richard said. "I saw her down in the lobby."

Chaz broke in. "Was Holly anywhere around?"

"Young? Dark hair?" Richard asked. "Pale, washed-out eyes?"

"I thought she was kind of pretty," Chaz replied. "A newer model along the lines of Myrna Loy."

"To each his own," Richard said dismissively. "She was hanging around trying to hear what Sudley was saying to Janey." He refocused his attention on Korine. "So, what did our dear friend the detective want with you?"

She caught him up. Richard was transformed completely when he grinned at her description of Sudley draped in the frilly pink nightie.

Korine smiled back. *So,* she thought, *he does have a sense of humor. Perhaps there's a reason to like him after all.*

Richard started to ask her a question, but Chaz stood up abruptly and asked, "Do you want me to leave the room so that you can tell him all about Leo?"

"I don't have anything else to add."

"Leo Gilcrest. High school. Richard needs to know."

Korine lifted her hand in protest, then let it drop. Chaz was right. "It turns out that Leo Gilcrest and I went to high school together. He's changed his name since then, so I didn't realize at first that Leo Gilcrest was the same boy I once knew. Oddly enough, we even went out once. What happened between the two of us was long, long ago, and it has nothing to do with Dodie's death."

Richard had returned to his previous formality. "Forgive me for saying this. I can't imagine anyone dating someone, then forgetting him so completely that you fail to recognize him later."

"I know it's hard to believe. I can give you lots of reasons why I didn't recognize him. But, basically, we only went out one time. Our families weren't from the same crowd." Korine swallowed hard once, then continued, "He left town right after we went out, and I never saw or heard from him again. I graduated from high school nearly forty years ago. How many people do you remember from your past, even just a couple of years back?"

She didn't tell them how she had spent a considerable amount of time listening to Dodie snore while she tried to escape the fact that Leo Gilcrest seemed uncomfortably familiar, even if she couldn't quite put her finger on the *why* of it at the time.

Korine stood up. "Now, if you're done grilling me, I'm going to hop into that massive decadent tub and wallow in my misery all alone for a while."

Neither of the men tried to stop her. As she shut the door, she heard Richard ask Chaz, "Have you talked to her yet?"

"No," her son responded. "The timing didn't seem right somehow."

Korine knew, as a mother, she should go back out and make them tell her what else they'd learned. Come to that, she still hadn't gotten Chaz to tell her what was on his mind out at the beach. She leaned back against the door and shut her eyes. A tear snaked its way down her cheek. She brushed her hand against it, impatient with herself for indulging in self-pity.

She hadn't even tried to get Chaz to talk with her since the day before, even though she'd had a window of opportunity that morning. She turned the water on. A bath would go a long way toward restoring her ability to listen. Then she'd tackle her son.

WHEN KORINE stepped out of her bedroom an hour later, the suite was deserted. A note on the bar from Chaz said that they had gone out for lunch and would catch up with her sometime mid-afternoon. He advised her to stay put, but she wasn't going to take that advice.

Picking up her purse, she hitched it on her shoulder and went out to catch the elevator. A moment later, the door opened and she stepped in. After the reaction she'd experienced that morning from Holly, Korine knew that the hotel was now off-limits. But not even murder could keep her from wandering Savannah.

Scurrying through the crush of people in the lobby, she stepped out into the sunshine. After a moment of hesitation, she turned right and began to stroll along the sidewalk. As she walked, Korine felt her troubles seem to peel off her shoulders.

A red light stopped her a block later. As she waited impatiently for the light to change, she knew she'd done the right thing. Across the street was one of the garden squares for which the city was famous. The light changed.

Strolling again at a leisurely pace, Korine reached the park and chose a shady path to wander. She sat on one of the benches, taking in the view. Sweeps of dark green grass vied with the colorful exotic shoots of hidden gingers and nodding heads of caladium under the shade trees. Closing her eyes, she began identifying scents. Heaven.

Dodie's face inserted itself into her daydreams. Not the antagonistic Dodie of real life, but the Dodie who, Korine firmly believed, had lived under her made-up skin and scraped-back hair. Korine's nightmare about Dodie came to mind again as she sat there in the park, chilled despite the hot summer sun.

Dodie opened their hotel room door. She shouted incoherently at someone. When she slammed the door, a hand punched through the wooden door, grabbed Dodie by the hair, and pulled her out through the hole. Korine went to open the door to help Dodie. It was stuck fast. Korine looked through the hole left behind by Dodie's passing and saw Dodie looking back at her. Dodie's expression was the one she had quickly hidden from Korine when Dodie fled into the bathroom on the morning of her death. Fear. Fear of friendship. Fear of letting anyone close to her. As if friendship would cause her death.

Korine shuddered and opened her eyes. A small boy with tousled black hair had stopped in front of her and was staring at her shivering form.

"What's wrong with her?" the boy asked his mother. Instead of answering, the young woman scooted the boy away. As they went, Korine heard her shush the child.

Does it show? Korine wondered. Could people really tell that she'd been involved in a murder? She stood and walked a little way away. Tucked in around some lovely old azaleas down a small fork in the crumbling brick path were some peacock gingers that Korine had never seen before. Their variegated leaves glowed softly in the reflected light from the fountain in the center of the park. Stooping, she plucked a dead leaf from the plant and twirled it between her fingers as she thought about the people she considered most likely to have killed Dodie.

Sharon certainly had a good motive. If the everyday Dodie was anything like the person she'd been with Korine, the only question would be, what took Sharon so long to kill her? Sharon's public accusations of Korine could cover for guilt, easily enough.

Then there was Holly. Lovely girl, but maybe she'd had enough of Dodie's ruining her mother's life. She was a botany major, not to mention the fact that everyone who grew up here in Savannah knows how poisonous oleanders are. Korine eyed one beautiful peach-colored specimen growing in front of a tall Federal-style home across the way. They were certainly plentiful enough here to make the poison very available. Yes, both Holly and Sharon were possibilities.

Then there was Leo.

Korine threw the mangled leaf on the ground and tried to stand. Her sleeve caught on a branch, and she turned to disentangle herself. Through the thin veil of the shrubbery in front of her, she caught a glimpse of two people from the conference.

"Do you suppose she really did it?" one of them asked.

"I've known Korine McFaile for a good many years, and I don't think she'd do anything of the sort. Dodie Halloran was no better than she looked. She deserved whatever it was that she got." Sallie Dunwoody, who had come to Pine Grove to do an article on Korine's gardens for *Magnolia's Gems* garden magazine three years before, drifted into view.

Korine felt a rush of gratitude that Sallie would stick up for her. She still hid until the two women had passed. Being glad that Sallie thought she was innocent, and being ready to talk with anyone, were two separate items.

Turning away, Korine abandoned the park. A few more blocks down the street was a restaurant. She turned in. Surely it was far enough from the hotel that she could get some real breathing space.

Once inside, she slid into a chair and opened the menu that the waitress gave her. Choosing the turkey club, Korine handed the menu back and settled down to wait.

Soon the waitress returned with the sandwich. Korine was just about to take a bite when she caught a glimpse of a familiar figure framed by the restaurant windows. Sharon, head down, was walking very fast. Frozen in place for a few seconds, Korine absently took a bite. As she swallowed, the club sandwich turned to dust in the back of her throat. Following Sharon, trying to look secretive while doing it, was J.J. Bascom.

Korine put the rest of the sandwich down on her plate, pulled out her wallet, and left enough money on the table to pay for her meal. Ignoring the waitress's startled questions, she flew out the door and tried to catch up with J.J.

"What the hell do you think you're doing?" was his greeting when she caught up to him.

"Same thing you are," Korine returned.

The two of them continued together in uncompanionable silence for a few blocks.

"What are we doing?" she asked after the two of them turned the corner to find Sharon going up the steps of the tall, slim, whitewashed brick house on the opposite corner.

J.J. stepped back against the wall of the building next to him and pulled Korine with him. "I was following her," he said, "because when she headed out of the hotel, she mentioned that she was mad enough to kill. Kind of an inflammatory statement to make following a murder."

Korine tore her gaze away from the empty stoop of Sharon's house. "Do you think she killed Dodie?"

"I don't know, but I like to know as much as I can about suspects when I'm—" He had the grace to look embarrassed.

"Yes?" Korine prompted. She almost smiled.

"Sudley told me this morning to keep out of it. I'm trying to."

"So you're just going to follow suspects, not talk to them?" she asked sharply.

"Don't be wise with me. I can't sit there in the lobby and watch people walk around and make a mess out of an investigation. Sudley's driving me nuts. When I introduced myself to him, would you believe he didn't even crack a smile? I wish I could borrow his face to play cards with Doc James next Thursday night. I'd make a mint of money."

"Do you think he knows what he's doing?"

"Probably." J.J. peered around the corner of the building and squinted in the direction of Sharon's house. "I just don't like his methods. Go on back to the hotel," he said dismissively. "I'll be back in a little while. I've got a few questions for you about Leo Gilcrest."

"You too? Does everyone know I once had a date with that man?"

"You might have mentioned you knew him. Did you know he broke off his engagement with Dodie over you?"

"No." Korine's eyes burned. "He couldn't have. I never knew where he'd gone. I haven't seen that man in thirty-seven years." She stopped and firmly shut the door on her memories before continuing. "I'm not going back to the hotel. I can't explain it, but Dodie seems to be haunting me. I've got to have something to do. I can't sit around moaning about the injustice of it all. How about I go over there and ask Sharon some questions? I'm not bound by some arcane policeman's creed of non-obstruction."

"Sure, you and Janey can open a detective agency instead of a landscaping firm. You won't make near as much money, though, because you're going to get yourselves killed poking your heads in things that people don't want disturbed." J.J. stopped, his face flushed with anger.

"Don't try and make me be reasonable," Korine argued.

Without warning, J.J.'s hand shot out and pulled Korine back. "She's leaving," he said.

Sure enough, Sharon had exited the house, slamming the door behind her. She climbed into a gold Mercedes parked by the curb and, tires squealing in protest, pulled away.

So much for anyone talking to her.

Korine turned to J.J. Now that Sharon was gone, there was nothing to keep her from trotting right up to the front door and knocking. She said so.

J.J. kept his grip on her arm. "No, let me do it."

She peered up at his face. He looked altogether too knowing for her. "What's going on here?" she asked. "You aren't just following Sharon for your own information, are you?"

J.J. tensed. Looking beyond Korine to Sharon's house, he sighed. "I wish you didn't see through people so well. Leo told me that Dodie had tried at one time to…," J.J. paused delicately, "become friendly with Sharon's husband. I followed Sharon because we thought it worthwhile to see the two of them together."

"Why can't we go in together?"

"There's nothing here that I can't do—alone—better than I can with you tagging along." J.J. spoke with finality.

Frustrated, Korine turned to walk away. She'd find Chaz and get him to talk to her. That, at least, would get her mind off Dodie. In parting, she said, "Fine, then I guess I don't need to tell you that those bushes peeking over the top of that lovely white wall surrounding their garden are oleander."

The look on J.J.'s face was its own reward.

ELEVEN

THE WINSLOWS' FRONT DOOR had a crack in the paint down near the bottom, as if the postman might be in the habit of kicking the door to announce the arrival of the mail as he slid the envelopes through the slot. J.J. looked for a doorbell. Failing to find one, he knocked.

Winslow answered the door. The shoulders of his suit jacket slumped. Sharon must have taken the stuffing out of her husband when she left. The man's eyebrows drew down as he took in the face of a stranger sitting on his front stoop. "We don't need any," the man said and tried to shut the door.

J.J. did the tried-and-true thing. He stuck his foot in the door. "Mr. Winslow, can I talk to you a bit about your wife's cousin Dodie?" he asked. "My name's J.J. Bascom. I'm the police chief back home. My wife's here at the conference with her partner, who was rooming with Dodie when she was killed."

The man's sturdy face didn't change expression as he looked J.J. over from head to toe. The impression of barely suppressed rage was, nevertheless, a strong one. "I don't think I have anything to say on the matter to you. Someone was here this morning, and until you show me a badge or a search warrant, I'm not letting anyone else in this house."

J.J. didn't think that a badge from Pine Grove would have a lot of influence with this man, so he didn't bother to fish it out of his pocket. Winslow used his own foot to dislodge J.J.'s from the doorway. The mail flap jingled in sympathy as Sharon's husband shut the door in his face.

Raising his hand, J.J. knocked again. He wasn't used to people shutting the door in his face, and he knew for sure he didn't like it. When Winslow didn't return to open the door, J.J. retreated down the few steps to the sidewalk.

The encounter had been interesting. He wondered what Winslow's profession was. Sharon's husband was able to hold his emotions in check pretty easily. A man like that wasn't going to tell a total stranger coming in off the street all his secrets, that was for darned sure.

J.J. was frustrated by his lack of credentials in this case. He was reassured, however, that the man had revealed something of interest, even if he hadn't meant to do so. Sudley was looking in more than one direction. Judging by Winslow's current anger level, the detective was looking assiduously enough to ruffle some feathers.

J.J. turned the corner and walked along the white-washed brick fence that screened the garden from the road. As he walked, he studied the plants peering over the top of the wall. Hot-pink blossoms tipped the long branches. Long slim leaves radiated around a woody branch. The fence was five feet tall, so the bushes had been trimmed here and there along the way to allow pedestrians some headroom. J.J. wondered how long ago the hedges had last been clipped. He'd have to ask Janey how long it took oleander leaves to dry enough to be able to crush them to powder.

It wouldn't take much, and every bit of that pretty plant was toxic. He remembered some campers near his dad's house on Galveston Island had picked some of the oleander branches to roast their hot dogs. Their bodies hadn't been pretty when they were discovered the next morning.

The next turn brought J.J. face to face with a sign announcing that the imposingly grand house behind it was the birthplace of Juliette Gordon Low, founder of the Girl Scouts of America. Stepping aside, he let a group of young girls go by. As they slipped by him, they talked excitedly about the tour they'd be taking there the following day.

If he and Janey had a girl, she'd wear one of those funny green uniforms, just like these scouts. J.J. smiled, thinking of a petite version of Janey, all big eyes and flying pigtails as she ran to greet him when he got home from work. He half-turned, watching the giggling schoolgirls round the corner and disappear from view. A girl would be nice.

As J.J. walked back to the hotel, he thought about what he knew—and what he suspected he knew. He wished that Sudley would be more forthcoming with his information. Getting it thirdhand through Chaz's friend was tiresome, at best.

Sharon was an odd one, that was for certain. She'd been upset, appropriately enough, when she found out Dodie was dead. Still, even discounting the Leo factor, the public nature of the accusations she'd made about Korine were unusually vehement. Either she knew something more about this than she'd revealed, or she was covering for someone.

There was the possibility that Dodie really had slipped by her cousin and gotten to George Winslow all those years ago. If Korine's high-school relationship with Leo was sufficient to consider her as a suspect, then an old relationship between Dodie and her cousin's husband would similarly brand Sharon. If Korine hadn't shown up, J.J. might have been able to get closer and listen under the open windows of the Winslow house while Sharon and her husband fought.

When J.J. arrived at the hotel, the first person he saw in the lobby was Sharon, talking quietly with her daughter by the escalators. Unfortunately, Sharon also saw him. By the time he made it across the lobby, she was on her way down, soon lost from view.

He started down after her but was stopped by the hard pressure of Holly's hand on his arm. "Leave my mother alone!"

Looking down into Holly's upturned face, J.J. decided he didn't want a girl after all. There was a big difference between the fresh, open faces of those Girl Scouts and the secrets that were buried in Holly's face. He couldn't read her emotions near as easily as he had read Winslow's. Women could hide too much under all that makeup.

"I'm not going to bother your mother," J.J. said.

"Sure, and following her all over town didn't bother her a bit. She saw you," Holly said spitefully. "If people would just leave her alone, she'd be all right." The girl's tone was more hopeful than certain.

"Your mom shouldn't be nervous. Unless she's got something to hide?"

Holly didn't answer right away. J.J. glanced down the escalator regretfully after Sharon. When he looked back up at Holly, he caught the tail end of an expression of fear as it crossed her face.

"Your wife's in there talking with Detective Sudley." Holly indicated the hotel business office behind the registration desk.

"How long has she been in there?" J.J. felt a little righteous anger of his own burn through his veins.

"About fifteen minutes, maybe more. He was looking for you first but then asked Janey if she would talk with him since you weren't around." Holly looked smug, as well she should, having gotten him all riled up.

Back home, he never would have let anyone involved in one of his cases see him squirm that way. But that was the point. It wasn't his case.

"You'd better go help your wife," Holly said.

Surprised by the spite he saw in those pretty blue eyes, J.J. said, "You sure take after your mother's side of the family, don't you? Your dad would have dug that barb in more smoothly."

Holly recoiled. "You talked to Daddy?"

"Your mom left home before I caught up to her. I

knocked, your dad answered. Interesting man." J.J. waited to see how Holly would take that bait.

"Daddy's not likely to have said 'boo' to you. Unless Detective Sudley deputized you." Her cool blue eyes searched J.J.'s face.

"Sudley is treating me just the same as anyone else in this case," he replied mildly.

Holly clasped the papers she held to her chest and said, "So you know how it feels. Just leave Mom alone." She glared at him and walked away.

J.J. watched her go. She was much more like her mother and Dodie than he'd previously thought. Inconsistent, mean-spirited, and irritating. He turned and made his way over to the office where Sudley was talking to Janey.

The scene that met J.J.'s eyes when he opened the door threatened his blood pressure once again. Sudley leaned over Janey, who was sitting as far back in her chair as she possibly could.

"Your friend could be in big trouble," Sudley was saying.

Janey frowned slightly, as if confused. "She didn't do anything."

"And neither did Janey," J.J.'s deep voice growled. He put his hand on her shoulder. She was like ice under her thin silk shirt. J.J. squeezed in sympathy, and her knotted muscles relaxed under his hand.

Sudley backed off. He stood up, eye to eye with J.J. It was clear that the detective was pleased to find himself the taller of the two by a good inch. "Of course not," he said. "Now that you're here, I have a few questions of my own for you. Have a seat." Sudley stacked up a sheaf of papers and put them to one side, then hitched up the leg of his pants and planted one hip on the corner of the desk.

J.J. remained standing. He didn't want this son of a gun towering over him. He knew all these tactics and didn't appreciate Sudley's using them against him. "What exactly do you think you're accomplishing here?" J.J. said. "I know that you've talked to the Winslows. Sharon's sufficiently upset enough that I know you weren't as gentle as you're trying to make us think. Korine has a motive smaller than a gnat. So why are you going after her?"

Sudley fiddled with a pen as he considered J.J. "I'm keeping an open mind. I'm sure you can appreciate the difficult position I'm in right now. You're one of us. Like it or not, you're connected to one of my strongest suspects. I can't exactly give you all the evidence that I have right now." He indicated the pile of reports he'd shoved aside. "Where were you yesterday morning?" Sudley asked.

"Around the corner, watching reruns of 'Bonanza.'" J.J. answered.

"And Mrs. McFaile?" Sudley turned to Janey.

J.J. took his wife's hand as it crept up to her shoulder. "Korine came up to my room around eight, then we went downstairs. I went looking for J.J., and Korine went on into the rose session."

"And what time was it when you met up with either Mrs. McFaile or your husband again?"

"I'm not sure." Janey bit her lip again.

Sudley made a note in his little book, then said, "Tell me about going into the room where Dodie was killed."

"Korine came up to my room early. We talked, then she went down to the conference, and I went to look for J.J."

"What did you two ladies talk about?" Sudley interrupted.

"In my room? About Dodie's manners mostly," Janey said. Her neck grew warm. Even with her coloring, J.J. could tell she was blushing. She hated to talk about people behind their backs, and this obviously came under that header.

"And when did you meet up with Mrs. McFaile again?"

"Like I said, I'm not sure of the time," Janey answered. "My watch is broken, so I haven't worn it this weekend. Nice for vacations. Not so convenient when you want to be able to truthfully defend a friend."

Sudley's gray eyes narrowed as he looked at Janey. A telltale crinkle appeared in the corner of one eye.

Hot dog! J.J. thought. *He's trying not to smile at her.*

"And whose idea was it to go into the room where Dodie was murdered?" Sudley asked.

"Korine's," Janey answered. "She was concerned about Dodie. That's how Korine is. She'll mother anyone."

"Mrs. McFaile told me how the stain on the tablecloth got onto her blouse. There was a similar stain on Leo Gilcrest's pants."

"It got there the same way. They were trying to get through the tangle of wires on the table, and they both brushed up against it. Leo got it on his hand and wiped it on his pants by accident."

A young uniformed officer stuck his head in the door. "Sir?" he said, voice cracking as if he'd only just that moment gone through puberty. "I need you now, sir."

"I've told you before to quit 'sirring' me, John. What is it?"

John shifted his eyes sideways at J.J. and Janey, came to a decision, and blurted out, "Sharon Winslow's started throwing up. She says someone poisoned her. Her daughter ran her over to the Emergency Room. They're pumping her stomach. Do you want to go over and talk with her, sir, or do you want one of us to go?"

Sudley stood up. "I'm afraid I'll have to finish with you later." He waited for Janey and J.J. to precede him out the door before closing it behind him. He followed the young officer at a run out the front door, leaving J.J. standing there wondering what to think about this turn of events.

J.J. looked back at the office door. The police reports on the desk in that closed room began to call to him.

"Don't you dare!" Janey exclaimed. "He's already told you you're out of your territory here."

"Jurisdiction," J.J. corrected mechanically. "Yeah, he told me where to get off." He moved over to the door anyway. "I think you left your purse inside."

"I did not!" Janey began, then quickly followed him inside as J.J. pushed the door and found that, in Sudley's haste, he had not locked the door behind him.

"You don't have any authority here," Janey said warningly.

"I know that. But I could always bring things to Sudley's attention."

"Would he consider them?"

"He may be biased, but I think he's honest." J.J. smiled tightly. Sudley was playing games with him and he didn't like it. A quick look wouldn't hurt anyone. He positioned Janey by the door and said, "Tell me if he's coming back."

Janey eased the door closed. "Are we going to go to jail if he catches us?" she asked nervously.

"No," J.J. replied shortly.

The postmortem report was brief and to the point: Death by oleander. According to stomach contents, the poison had been given to Dodie in a Bloody Mary.

"I wonder if he's taken samples of the bushes outside Sharon's home," J.J. mused. Riffling through the lab reports, he found that Sudley had, in fact, done just that. J.J. pulled out the page on Korine's seed packet. There was only one set of prints on the packet. In J.J.'s experience, nothing ever had only one set of clear prints. There should have been others, partials from someone who had handled it before it came into Korine's possession. Sudley wouldn't have missed those implications either. Someone was trying to frame Korine for Dodie's death.

"The coast is clear," Janey said, only half joking.

J.J. stood up and went over to the door. Putting his arm around his wife, they scooted out the doorway together.

"So, who do we need to talk with next?" Janey asked.

"You mean, who should I talk with," J.J. corrected.

"We," Janey repeated firmly. "Korine needs all the help that we can give her."

J.J. slipped her hand into his. He felt her shiver as he said, "If someone has poisoned two people, then they're not going to hesitate to kill whoever gets in their way. You stay out of this."

"I understand how you feel," Janey said.

"Good. Then stay out of it. No Holly. No Leo. No Sharon. Go find Korine. Try and keep her from doing anything stupid. You can keep each other out of trouble."

Janey glared at him. "What are you going to do?"

"Go talk to Leo. I'd like to know where he's been all day long." He gripped Janey's elbow. "Honey, I mean it. You're way too important to me to risk letting some idiot murderer have a chance to get rid of you. Leave it to the experts."

Janey looked at him, her love lending shine to her eyes. He leaned over and pulled her into his shoulder. They walked over to the elevator and J.J. turned her loose. He waited until she was safely inside, Korine's floor button pushed.

It wasn't until J.J. was on the escalator headed downstairs, all set to find Leo Gilcrest to ask him where he'd been all morning, that J.J. realized that once again, he'd let his wife get away without promising him anything at all.

TWELVE

KORINE WALKED THROUGH nearly all of Savannah's famous squares on her circuitous route back to the hotel. There was a lot to think about. The only conclusion she reached was that she could not put off talking to Chaz any longer. Her son, and her relationship with him, were far more important than anything else that had happened that weekend. She brushed aside a dangling pink blossom from an out-of-control crepe myrtle outside the hotel and went through the revolving doors.

Using the house phone in the lobby, Korine called her room. No answer. She hung up, switched to the pay phone, and dialed Chaz's apartment. The machine picked up.

"Chaz, are you there?" She waited, then said, "Honey? I'm back at the hotel. I need to talk with you. Can we meet for dinner? My treat." Korine hung up the phone. She swung around, heart pounding, when someone laid a hand on her shoulder. It was Janey.

"Where have you been?" Janey asked. "I've been looking all over for you. Sharon's gone to the hospital—poisoned—and J.J. can't take it that this isn't his case, so he's wandering around acting like a spy."

Korine ignored the concern behind Janey's statement about J.J., for the moment, in her shock. "Sharon's been poisoned?"

"According to one of the policemen. I guess that means she didn't kill Dodie."

Korine's heart constricted. "Who would want to kill Sharon?"

"Not you. That's for sure," Janey replied. She searched Korine's face with compassionate brown eyes. "Let's get out of here. It's not far down to the river. There are several good restaurants there. We can walk." Putting one arm around her friend, Janey steered a resistant Korine back out into the warm sunshine.

Korine protested, "I've just this minute left a message for Chaz, telling him to call me in my room."

"You don't know when Chaz will get home," Janey pointed out in response to Korine's protests. "You've already asked him for dinner, right?"

"I was going to wait in my room," she repeated stubbornly.

"Sitting up there isn't going to get Chaz to call any sooner. Dinnertime is a few hours away. Come and relax a little."

"I suppose you're right." Korine gave in to Janey's gentle pressure on her shoulders and walked the way Janey was pushing her to go. They walked down and crossed East Bay Street into Emmet Park.

"Does J.J. know if they really suspect me?" Korine asked.

"He doesn't think so," Janey answered.

Conversation ceased while they negotiated the steep stairs down to the river road. The slope of the road beside them was surfaced in old paving stones, ship's ballast from the time of Savannah's birth. Emerging onto a cracked and narrow sidewalk, the two women followed it until they came to a small pub whose menu caught their eye.

The dark interior suited Korine's mood. The host placed them in the back, at a table supported by a wooden barrel, and left to go fetch their drink orders.

"If Sharon was poisoned, and I'm not guilty, then who does that leave?" Korine asked. "And don't tell me Leo. What twisted reason could he have for wanting Sharon out of the way? Holly is more likely. You said yourself that Sharon was horribly overprotective. That girl has been caught between those two women all her life."

"I refuse to believe that Holly had anything to do with this," Janey said firmly.

Impatiently, Korine blurted out a rebuttal. "I know that you like her, and she does seem nice enough, but it's either Holly or Leo. And Leo just doesn't have the motive to get rid of Sharon that Holly does."

Janey didn't reply at first, looking away and gripping her bottom lip between her teeth as she struggled to frame a reply.

Korine felt guilty. She hadn't meant to take out her fear and anger on Janey. She dropped her head into her hands, only to realize that they were sticky with residue from the table. Korine wiped the offending film from her fingers with her napkin and apologized. "I'm sorry. I want to break something. But not our friendship."

Janey hesitated before answering. "We can guess all we want, but we can't know. I'm tired of even thinking about it. Let's talk about something else, like that wild project Sarah Jane is trying to talk you into with the Morton place."

Korine made an attempt to smile and said, "Sarah Jane. Now there's a woman who defines *difficult*. She's still thinking of putting the plantation into production—and in tea, of all things. She even made me promise to go up and tour the Charleston Tea Plantation, which is not even in Charleston, thank you very much, but on some island south of Charleston."

Remembering the total failure of that side trip gave Korine an infusion of badly needed humor. "It was beautiful," she continued, "and I can understand what impressed Sarah Jane about it. But she doesn't realize how much work is involved. The look on the face of the owner when I told him why I'd stopped by—priceless! This man has a four-year degree from tea-tasting school in London. Who is Sarah Jane going to get to volunteer for that one? Tea is harvested every two weeks. This place has a custom tea harvester, the only one in existence. If I'd even wanted to try this venture, the thought of trying to duplicate what they've got going was enough to talk me out of it."

"It's not the best idea Sarah Jane's ever had," Janey said, the closest thing to a catty comment she would make.

Korine nearly snorted with laughter at the understatement. "You can't force something to grow in an area where it's not meant to thrive. And evidently, the camellia species that tea comes from needs the southern climate to produce. But you know Sarah Jane. Once she gets an idea, she thinks it's as good as done."

"Speaking of thriving, Pine Grove is a good place to raise children," Janey said.

"You're pregnant again?" Korine exclaimed. She looked Janey up and down. She did have that glow about her.

"Not yet—at least that I know of—but wish us luck. According to my thermometer, I'll be taking a very tired J.J. back home with me."

Korine laughed outright this time. It felt so good that she was immediately ashamed.

Janey caught Korine's hesitation. "You don't have to mourn constantly, you know. Especially not for someone you hardly knew, and liked even less. That's one of the things I admire the most about you. You don't have a hypocrite's bone in your body."

"Thank you." Korine was warmed by Janey's words. "Do you want a boy or a girl?"

"Boy. They have an easier life, I think, than women do. More choices anyway."

"What about J.J.?" Korine smiled at the waiter as he brought their soup and sandwiches. This was her second lunch of the day, even if it was mid-afternoon. She'd walked out on the first meal and was ravenous.

"He told me this morning he wants a girl. Little does he know," Janey said, with a wry twist to her mouth. "You've raised a boy. Would you rather have had a girl?"

The contents of Korine's sandwich dropped onto her plate, leaving her holding two empty slices of bread. Trying to reassemble the sandwich with shaking fingers, she swallowed hard. "No," she said to her plate. "I wouldn't trade Chaz for anything in the world."

"I've said something wrong." Janey's soft voice cut through the searing pain in Korine's head.

Worried fingers shredded the bread into useless crumbs of dough. Korine held her breath, knowing that if she inhaled, she would begin to cry. Janey's brown hands reached in and took the disintegrating crust out of Korine's fingers. Janey trapped Korine's cold hands in her own warm palms. Korine looked at Janey.

"Chaz told you," Janey said.

Startled, Korine frowned. "He's told you already?"

"I knew," Janey said.

"How can you know?" How could Janey, who had never held that tiny infant boy in her arms and nursed him through everything from scarlet fever to football injuries, know what was a total mystery to Chaz's own mother. "I don't know, and this weekend has been so horrible—what with Dodie's death—that he hasn't had time to tell me. Chaz said he's not dying. What else is there that's so bad?"

"I'm sorry." Janey dropped Korine's hands in her distress. "It's not my news to tell. I had hoped he'd spoken with you already."

"Is it me?" Korine asked, casting about for something

to latch onto. Janey's words were confusing. "Have I done something to hurt him?"

Janey leaned both elbows on the table and looked at Korine directly. "Not yet." Those steady brown eyes wouldn't let Korine look away. Korine saw pity shining in Janey's eyes. That shook her; she couldn't bear pity.

Janey continued, "Sometimes you have to set the transplants out and let them harden off on their own. Let him go be his own person, Korine. He can't find his dreams when he's busy trying to fulfill yours."

"I don't believe I've asked him to." Korine was suddenly angry.

Janey sat steady next to Korine. "But he might think you have."

"I'm not hungry." For the second time that day, Korine left a sandwich sitting uneaten on her plate as she grabbed her purse and walked away from the confusion created by Janey's words.

Alone, Korine turned right after leaving the pub and walked blindly down the wooden walkway to the end of the block. She stumbled going down the steps to the street, saved from injury by the kindness of a stranger who caught her elbow before she could fall. Brushing away tears, Korine continued quickly down the street, ignoring Janey's calls behind her. A block later, Janey was still behind her.

Korine turned and waited for Janey to catch up. She apologized. "I don't know what's come over me. This weekend was supposed to be a break. It's become hell on earth."

Janey slipped an arm around Korine's shoulders and

they walked on together. The river ran by on their left, the water constantly shifting shape and direction. The two of them stopped to watch a barge go by, beginning a journey out to sea. A silvery fish sounded not a foot in front of her, and Korine jumped as if it had slapped her. She took a step away from the edge and turned away. Janey turned with her.

In front of them stood a statue of a waving girl. She faced downstream, greeting each ship that came up to the port. Korine went over to read the inscription on the plaque. It told the story of Florence Martus, whose seafaring sweetheart had never returned. Local legend had it that the girl's promise to wait for her lover led her to welcome every ship back into port, ever hoping that her beloved would return. Her constancy was commemorated by this statue.

Korine looked up. That constancy had gotten Florence a statue. She felt a stab of sympathy for the long-dead woman. She had waved for many years, yet the girl's sweetheart had never returned. Korine turned to Janey and smiled tentatively.

"You feeling better?" asked Janey.

"A little," Korine replied. "I've been wallowing, haven't I?"

"A little." Janey smiled. "You're entitled to a few minutes of it every day. Didn't anyone ever tell you that?"

"Can't say as I recommend it," Korine retorted.

Turning away from the river, the pair climbed the hill to the park at the top. Passing a pair of homeless men sitting on a wrought-iron park bench, they got to the street corner opposite the hotel and punched the WALK button. A minute later, they entered the hotel.

HER PHONE LIGHT was blinking when Korine entered the room. One message, from Richard. She picked up the phone and dialed his office.

"What is it?" Janey asked.

"I'm on hold," Korine responded, just as Richard picked up.

"Sorry about that," he said. "We heard about Sharon, and were concerned about you."

"We?" Korine repeated blankly.

"Chaz and I," Richard replied impatiently. "Are you doing all right?"

"Fine," Korine lied. She wrinkled her nose at Janey and got a puzzling look back.

Richard said, "Listen, we got your message about dinner. We'll pick you up around six?"

Korine was beginning to hate Richard's royal *we* as much as she hated Sudley's rhetorical questions. "Yes, but—"

Richard interrupted, "Good, we'll see you then." And he hung up the phone.

Giving Janey the look of pure fury she wanted to level at Richard, Korine dropped the receiver in its cradle. The phone rang. Regarding it like she would a striking snake, Korine cautiously reached out and picked it back up again. "Hello?"

"Good, you're there." J.J.'s booming voice came over the wire. "Did Janey find you?"

"She's right here." Korine handed the phone to Janey, then went over to the window and traced patterns in the condensed moisture while the couple talked.

"What did you say?" Janey exclaimed.

Korine turned around. Janey was standing, one hand on hip, as if scolding an invisible J.J. in front of her. Janey told Korine, "Sharon told Sudley that she thinks you poisoned her. Evidently, a box of chocolates came to her room this morning, supposedly from you."

"I never sent anything!" Korine said. She pointed at the extra phone and raised her eyebrows in a mute request. Janey nodded her approval and Korine picked up the extension on the bar.

"No prints on the box that match Korine's. That's good, right?" Janey's nose wrinkled as she listened to J.J.'s response, then said, "That doesn't make any sense."

"What?" Korine said. She'd missed what J.J. had said.

"The prints on the inside of the box were Dodie's," J.J. repeated. "But the note is definitely in Korine's handwriting."

"I left a note for Dodie Saturday morning," Korine said. "Something about mending fences and let's give each other another try."

J.J. spoke to someone on the other end of the phone. "Yep," he said. "That's it."

"How did Dodie send candy after she was dead?" Janey asked.

"Messenger service had been holding it and delivered it this morning as instructed. The boy identified Dodie from a picture."

Korine exclaimed, "If Dodie did this, then maybe she killed herself and is trying to frame me!"

"That's a little too far out there," J.J. cautioned.

"What does Sudley have to say about this?" Janey asked.

"Let's just say he's a lot more friendly now than he was an hour ago. He still wants me to keep clear of the investigation, but he did listen to what I had to say about the Winslow family dynamics. I haven't tried running actual theories by him yet."

Male voices swelled in the background. J.J. said something to one of the men on his end, then spoke again to Janey. "Listen, I'd better go. Stick close to Korine, will you? Just don't eat anything that shows up at the door."

"I promise," Janey replied. "And J.J.?"

"Yes." His wary voice came back over the line.

"Don't forget what my thermometer said about tonight." Janey's tone held equal parts warning and amusement.

Korine hung up to let them finish their conversation in private, but not before she caught J.J.'s reply.

"Already?" he said. "Your thermometer said the same thing yesterday morning. I thought we were supposed to rest a day or so in between."

"Sometimes you've got to do things off the record to keep things fresh. We hit the thermometer timing yesterday. Today's for fun."

How could Janey joke about sex at a time like this? Korine looked at her incredulously. When she saw the look on her friend's face, Korine's anger faded. Janey's expression held five parts anxiety for each measure of teasing good humor. She was using this as bait to get J.J. to leave well-enough alone. His snort of laughter in response to Janey's outrageous statement was audible from across the room. Janey's tension eased as she joined in.

Korine remembered when she had been able to laugh like that with Charlie. Once upon a time, the boy who had grown into Leo Gilcrest had been able to make her laugh like that, as well. Turning her back on the pair, Korine traced her earlier design in the window and felt old beyond her years. Old, and alone.

THIRTEEN

J.J. HUNG UP the hotel wall phone and regarded it. So, Janey wasn't above bribery to get her own way. Shaking his head, he rejoined Sudley. "Korine wrote Dodie a note Saturday morning," he said. "Sounds like the one you found with Sharon's chocolates."

"It fits." Sudley scratched his eyebrow and stared out the window. "I sure wish I could figure out why Dodie sent those things to Sharon and why her timing had to be today. She'd arranged for that damn messenger service too carefully, and the ID is dead positive."

"So to speak," J.J. said.

Sudley grinned, making him look as nearly human as J.J. had seen to date.

"Korine asked if Dodie could have killed herself," J.J. said, allowing a wistful note to creep into his voice. Would that it could be that easy.

"Yeah, I suppose so," Sudley returned. "And then she threw up all over a tablecloth, stopped breathing, folded up the dirty tablecloth and put it in the bin, washed her face, climbed in the linen cart, put her hands on her chest, and buried herself in napkins."

"I knew that," J.J. said defensively.

Sudley studied his shoes, then glanced up sharply at J.J. from beneath drawn brows. "I can't ask you for help. It's just not done that way around here. I'm going to have to ask you to steer clear for a while longer."

"I see," J.J. said, even while he met Sudley's oblique look. "I have a confession to make. I went back and looked at your reports in the office."

"And you think I didn't know?" Sudley replied.

J.J. stood, regarding the detective. He wasn't sure exactly what this man was up to. Whatever it was, it hadn't been covered by anything he'd run across so far in his career in law enforcement. Sudley obviously wanted J.J.'s help, but he was going about it in the most confusing manner possible. Still, what he'd just said enabled J.J.'s conscience to clear about sneaking around after Sudley. J.J. would give the man the help he wasn't asking for but obviously wanted. It would be off the record, unofficial, and undocumented. That worked for J.J. As long as Sudley ceased warning him off every two seconds, all the while expecting J.J. to ignore that message.

"Do you suppose the two things are connected?" J.J. asked.

"I couldn't say. I've sent those chocolates off for analysis. It's entirely possible from Sharon's symptoms that they contain the same poison used to kill Dodie."

"Dodie could have been working with someone."

"Yeah," Sudley said again. He looked past J.J.'s shoulder to the lobby desk. Jutting out his chin, he said, "If your wife wasn't close to Mrs. McFaile—who at the time was my best suspect—I wouldn't have had to question Janey."

"If it weren't Janey, I would understand," J.J. said. It was as close as he could come to accepting Sudley's near-apology.

"Don't be a stranger," Sudley said and stuck his hand out. J.J. took it and nodded. The detective then walked over to the phone that J.J. had used and picked it up.

J.J. left Sudley to his work and went over to the desk. He saw Leo Gilcrest and cleared his throat.

Leo swung around. "What the hell is going on here?" he demanded. "Sharon's in the hospital, Holly's missing, and this idiot—" Leo indicated the young man behind the granite counter "—won't tell me where Korine is so that I can see if she's okay or not."

"As near as I know, Korine's just fine. Do you have any reason to believe that she might be in danger?" J.J. studied the man. Leo's forehead glistened with sweat in the glare of the hotel lighting. His color wasn't very good either. Definitely showing signs of stress.

"Where is she?"

"Sharon's gone to the hospital, I don't know which one. Holly's probably with her, though."

"No—Korine!" Leo's anger threatened to send him over the edge. With fists clenched at his side, he looked at the end of an invisible tether.

J.J. regarded this emotional outburst with interest. "Korine? She's with my wife."

The desk clerk, who was still unrepentantly eavesdropping, said, "You see why I didn't want to give out any information? Aside from being against the rules, this guy is nuts!"

Leo glared at the young man, who threw his glare right back at him. Leo pulled on J.J.'s arm and took a few steps to the side out of earshot.

"Where have you been all day?" J.J. asked.

"Meeting with clients. Sharon and I talked it over after most of the morning sessions were deserted. We cancelled everything as of this afternoon. I got back from my last meeting to find the police wasting their time searching my room. They won't tell me any details, just that Sharon went to the hospital. They all but told me to cool my heels here until they're done."

"What are they looking for in your room?"

"You're a police officer, suppose you tell me."

"I'm not on the Savannah police force," J.J. pointed out. "I don't know what they're looking for precisely. How are you so certain that they're wasting their time if you don't know what they're looking for?"

"I don't carry a box full of rat poison or anything with me, if that's what you're suggesting!" Leo answered hotly.

J.J. took stock of the situation. No getting around it, Leo Gilcrest was badly frightened. The man was definitely hiding something. J.J. said, "You've got an alibi for today, assuming that your clients back you up. What about Saturday morning?"

"I was in and out of all the conference rooms, including the one where Dodie was killed. People saw me, but I didn't go around saying, 'It's 11:15 and can you make a note of the time because I'll need an alibi later.' Holly was with me much of the time, so I suppose she can vouch for me. As for where Dodie was killed, Korine and your wife were already in that room when I got there. I'll swear that on the Bible if that's what you want." He even sounded sincere, which J.J. discounted. All successful criminals knew how to lie.

"Korine's been implicated, right?" Leo continued. "The only person I know who dislikes—disliked—Korine enough to do something that spiteful is—was—Dodie."

"Go on," J.J. said.

"There's no chance that Dodie killed herself, is there?"

J.J. saw real hope in Leo's eyes when he didn't answer right away. Then he answered firmly, "Dodie was murdered. Then somebody planted evidence on Korine that made it look like she was the one who poisoned Dodie.

"I've got another question," he continued. "This one's personal. You've been out of Korine's life for thirty-some-odd years, yet here you are acting like the recipient of love's first arrow. How do I know you didn't kill Dodie so that she'd leave you alone to pursue Korine?"

"You don't; I do. I was just about to go up and see Korine and talk about that very thing when you came up."

"You were about to go see her, but you had to ask the desk clerk, and then me, where she was?"

"I would have called first to see if she's in her room. Asking you was faster at the time," Leo said.

"Go on," J.J. said, pointing over to the house phones. "Call her. If Korine wants to see you, she'll tell you how to get up to her room." Out of the corner of his eye, he saw the desk clerk still avidly watching them as he helped another hotel guest. He'd have a talk with that young man later. His eye was too sharp; it was possible that he'd seen something that might be of interest in the investigation.

Leo reached into his hip pocket and, with an imperious gesture, pulled out a tooled-leather wallet. "I want to show you something," he said. He pulled out a dog-eared clipping and handed it to J.J. "You asked why I'm pursuing Korine so strongly. I found this clipping in a magazine the week my wife died. You said you thought I was acting like a lovesick puppy. Well, you're about right. Korine was the first girl I ever loved, and the timing seemed pretty much meant, seeing this about Korine just after Fiona died." Leo stopped, watching the lobby blindly while J.J. read the article.

It was the last one done on Korine's garden before the three women had started their landscaping company. It mentioned that Korine had trouble keeping the garden up after her husband died. Using before and after pictures, the magazine had shown the way Korine had let parts of it go back to the wild, softening the lines for a less formal, but still beautiful setting. The article had been folded to reveal a picture taken of Korine sitting on her porch, a tumble of roses framing her as she sat stroking her gray tabby cat. She smiled into the camera, house proud as usual of the mad profusion of color surrounding her.

"I waited a year. Then I called. I hung up when I heard her speak." Leo's voice was strained as he folded the article carefully the way it had been and slipped it back in his wallet. "I loved her for years, even after I moved. I wrote her every day for a while."

"Did she ever write back?" J.J. asked bluntly.

Leo leaned forward, resting his elbows on his knees as he examined the calluses on his palms. "No, she didn't. I don't think I really expected her to. She was one of the best girls at that school. I couldn't believe it when she said she'd go out with me in the first place. When I didn't hear from her, I figured she'd thought better of going out with someone from my side of town."

"So, even though she didn't write you back all those years ago—and even though Korine's repeatedly told you that she doesn't want anything to do with you now—you're still going to pursue her?" J.J. asked.

"That's not the way it is," Leo protested.

J.J. leaned forward. "Well, you'd better tell me how it is, then, because until you do, I'm going to do my level best to keep the two of you apart." He met Leo's angry gaze squarely, not backing down one inch from that hot stare.

"Honest, anyway, aren't you?" Unexpectedly, Leo grinned. "I wouldn't like you as well if you weren't protective." He sat back in his chair. The nervous sheen on his face was still there, but he seemed more at ease than he had earlier. "I'll tell you what," Leo said. "I'll trust you and your wife to protect Korine. But, if anything happens to her, then I'll have your hide as well as the hide off whoever hurts that lady."

"Big of you, considering you don't have a choice," J.J. replied. Even more unexpected than Leo's sudden ease, was J.J.'s response to him. He didn't want to trust this man. He stood and looked down at Leo Gilcrest. "Until Korine says otherwise, I'm going to help her keep her privacy. You're welcome to call her; but if she says to leave her alone, then leave her alone or *I'll* have *your* hide."

As J.J. strode across the lobby and hit the elevator button, he saw Leo go over to the phones and lift one and put it to his ear. J.J. got into the elevator, and Leo saluted him as the door closed. Damn character. Now he'd have to go up and talk to Korine and find out just what it was that she really wanted to do about Leo.

Before J.J. went up, though, he went down to the conference level. He wanted to see if he could catch up with Sudley before he went home for the night—if he went home for the night. J.J. hadn't told Janey that staying out of this investigation wasn't as much about territory and proving himself to the big-city detective as an inescapable urge to follow the scent. Yes, protecting Korine was a big factor in his decision to try and get Sudley to let him work with him on the case. But, the truth of it was that the chase itself could be pretty damn intoxicating.

Walking around the corner, he found Sudley deep in conversation with two uniformed officers. He hung back until they were done, then went over and said to the detective, "Gilcrest is hiding something and isn't very happy that you were searching his room."

"He shouldn't be very happy. He doesn't have any poisons, but he sure has a dossier on your friend. Pictures of her all over. She must be famous to have that many articles written about her house and garden."

J.J.'s heart constricted. "So much for the smarmy story he just told me." Quickly he ran over the article that Leo kept in his wallet and the story he told of their youthful involvement.

"That's more than I've been able to get either of them to tell me," Sudley said in disgust. "Korine referred me to Gilcrest, he referred me right back again. Are you sure an old busted romance is all there is to that relationship?"

As unofficial help, J.J. had the luxury of selecting what he would and wouldn't report. He wanted to talk with Korine first, then mull things over before he shared his suspicions. Instead of responding to Sudley's question, he said, "Gilcrest also mentioned the possibility that Holly was missing. Have you seen her since Sharon went to the hospital?"

"The girl rode in the ambulance with her mother," Sudley replied. "She was the one who called the paramedics, probably saved Sharon's life. I don't think she's missing, but I'd better call and find out. I'd rather know right away if we've got a third victim or not."

"I'm going to go up and talk with Korine for a bit."

"You do that. And then make up your mind if you're going to be impartial, or if I'm going to have to discount everything you have to tell me. If Korine McFaile didn't have a pretty strong alibi, she wouldn't be out of the running. As it is, Gilcrest and Holly are each other's alibis, and Sharon doesn't have one at all. Guess who'd be at the top of my list if she hadn't been poisoned?"

"I hear you," J.J. said. "I'll talk with Korine and see if she can shed some light on Leo Gilcrest."

"You do that," Sudley repeated.

The men went up the escalator in silence. They split

up and went their separate ways as they got to the top. J.J. walked past the hotel desk clerk and made a mental note of his name. He'd talk with Javier later. He wasn't in the mood right then. Time to confront Korine and make her tell him exactly why she acted like a long-tailed cat in a room full of rocking chairs every time Leo Gilcrest's name came up. He knew that Korine hadn't killed anyone, but whatever secret she was hiding might provide a clue that would help unravel the mystery that was Leo Gilcrest.

FOURTEEN

THE RESTAURANT WASN'T what Korine had in mind. Sandwiched in between Chaz and Richard, she helped herself to the overflowing basket of corn bread. As soon as she passed it along the row of people on their side of the table, Chaz put another bowl full of home-style cooking down in front of her. Why had she thought talking to him over dinner would be easier?

Richard had told her that this family-style restaurant was on the not-to-be-missed tour of Savannah, and since they knew that she needed distraction, it would be just the ticket. It was. A one-way ticket to slow-cooker hell. Although, there was a good side to this. She might never have to talk to Chaz at all. If the suspense of waiting until they got home and could actually talk didn't kill her, the liberal fat content in the food would surely do the job.

"Sudley finally saw reason," Richard was saying on her left, "when I pointed out that you couldn't be attending a session with a hundred and forty other people—at least half of whom are willing to testify on your behalf—and be in the room next door killing Dodie at the same time."

Meanwhile, Chaz, on her right, was not talking at all.

Every now and then he'd look over her head at Richard, then turn back to his meal. Occasionally, when he thought she wasn't looking, Chaz would sneak a glance at her, like he was measuring her mettle. After the events of the weekend and in her present frame of mind, it wasn't much. They each had things they needed to say to one another. After dinner, they would talk.

Desperate for something innocuous to say, Korine said, "Marlene makes corn bread like this." J.J.'s dispatch clerk back home was an outstanding cook.

"I don't need a woman who can cook. Besides," Chaz said, "isn't she getting married to Doc James?"

Exasperated that she had somehow been relegated to the role of Matchmaking Mother, something she had bent over backwards never to do, Korine snapped out, "Yes, she is getting very happily married to Darryl James. I wouldn't break up that relationship, even for your benefit."

Chaz carefully folded his napkin and laid it on the table next to his plate. Placing both hands on the edge of the table, he stared at his plate as if it held the secrets of the universe. "I'll be back shortly," he said. "I feel an urge of nature coming on."

Richard put a hand out to stop him. When Chaz brushed by him, unseeing, Richard pulled it back. A sigh rumbled in his throat, and he said, "That wasn't the best thing you could have said to him right now, you know." He swirled his spoon through a pile of mashed potatoes, sending a wave of gravy over the edge of his plate. "Between Leslie and me, and—"

"I'm sorry," Korine said bitterly. She turned in her chair to look directly at Richard's face. "I really didn't mean to insult you."

"I know," he said gently. "Chaz is just very sensitive about your opinion."

"I've noticed. Much more so than usual. Thank you," Korine said wryly, "for not taking it the wrong way. Everything I've said to Chaz so far this trip has been wrong." She smiled tentatively.

Richard was a difficult man to figure. At once grave and reserved, he had a knack for being generously tactful when it came to her relationship with her son. Chaz was fortunate in his choice of friends.

After a pause that was a heartbeat too long, Korine said, "You and Leslie had been together for a long time. It must be very painful."

"Yes." Richard took the next dish that was coming around from Korine and passed it to the person on his left, before turning back to resume their conversation. "Leslie has been unfaithful before, but this time—I just couldn't take it anymore. I packed Leslie's things up and changed the locks. Chaz moved down just in time to help me deal with the aftermath."

Korine tried to keep her surprise from appearing on her face. This was a new side of the story. Chaz had told her only that Richard had found someone else, not that Leslie had also been at fault. In Korine's mind, it made all the difference in the world. "The aftermath?" she prompted.

Richard shrugged the question away. "Eat that ham before it gets cold. I'm going to check on Chaz."

"Can I ask you something first?" she asked suddenly.

"Sure," he said, only slightly annoyed as he slid back into his chair.

Korine continued with difficulty. "I was glad when Chaz got the job down here. Not that I didn't love having him at home," she added hastily when she saw surprise stretch Richard's mouth into a grin. "I thought perhaps it was too cloistering, being underfoot at home."

Richard, still smiling slightly, made noncommittal go-on noises.

"But Chaz isn't any happier here. I can see that, at any rate. There's something I have to talk about with him, but the timing couldn't be worse."

"What is it that you want to talk to him about?" Richard asked.

"Something I should have told him a long time ago," Korine equivocated. "I kept waiting for the right time. Things were going well, and I thought I'd wait and enjoy that time. Then, last summer, Chaz changed."

"What happened?"

"He hasn't talked to you about this?"

"A little bit, but I'd like to hear it from you."

Richard and Korine looked up, startled, when the table burst into song. The woman sitting at the end was turning ninety. It was so far removed from the intense conversation that the pair of them were attempting to have, that Korine wanted to scream. She'd actually forgotten that they'd been placed at a table with another family.

Korine said, "Do you mind if Chaz and I go back to

his place after we finish? It's way past time for us to talk. Something's on his mind, and something's on mine. It's time to exchange these damn secrets and get them out in the open."

"I agree with you on that one," Richard said.

Out of the corner of her eye, Korine saw Chaz emerge from the men's room. "There he is."

"He's a grown man," Richard said in a carefully neutral tone. His eyes held a mute warning that Korine knew she needed to heed.

"He's my only child." She stopped and turned to face Richard's grave brown eyes again. "I know I'm more protective than I should be. I can't stop being his mother, even though he's grown up. It's a job for life, not just an eighteen-year stint."

Richard smiled. "As long as you know what you're doing, and that you remember that it's a son's job to pull away from that maternal tether, you'll both do fine. Specifically, don't try to fix him up with anyone. He's found his match." Richard ignored her astounded expression and pointed over her shoulder. "Here he comes, play like normal." Richard scowled playfully at her, which made her laugh.

"Are you all right?" Both Korine's breathless alto and Richard's baritone voiced the question at the same time.

"You should sing duets," Chaz said. "I'm fine." He took his seat and helped himself to some more fried chicken as it came around. "Did Richard tell you about that seed packet they found from your purse?"

"I thought that made me look *more* guilty, not less," Korine said.

"Actually, no," Chaz said. "Sudley said that he was pretty sure that whoever killed Dodie put it in your purse to make it look like you'd done it."

"So Sudley is my new best friend?" Korine said lightly. "Not likely, after the way he treated me."

"I don't think he's interested in you as a friend," Chaz said. "Maybe another sort of relationship."

Korine brushed that comment off with the consideration it deserved. No policeman worth his mettle would even consider anything of the sort. "That's one of the reasons I wanted to have dinner with you," Korine said. "To talk about relationships, I mean. Ours in particular."

Chaz looked over at Richard, as if for approval. "Do you really want to talk about this here and now?" he asked his mother.

The answer, of course, was no. This restaurant was wonderful if you wanted to meet a large number of people, enjoy their special occasions, and eat yourself silly; but that wasn't what Korine had in mind. "No," she answered. "I don't."

Richard stepped in. "Korine suggested that you two go back to the apartment and talk for a while. I've got some more work to do in the office. So, if you don't mind, I'll be running along."

"Mother," Chaz said after a moment of stunned silence. "What Richard obviously hasn't told you is that I'm staying in his apartment. We can't exactly kick him out while we talk." He thought about it for a second, then added slowly, "But you're probably right, the apartment is a good idea."

The person on Chaz's far side, part of the family of birthday revelers, tapped him on the arm and passed him a basket. Chaz looked down inside and stuck his hand in. It emerged with a green and purple circus-style party hat.

"That's appropriate," he said shortly and shoved the basket back into the startled hands of the man who had given it to him in the first place. Standing, Chaz walked away from the table. Korine and Richard didn't hesitate to follow his example. She had never felt less like celebrating.

The three of them walked out into the night after settling the bill. The branches of the live oaks along the road formed a leafy bower. Moonlight slipping through the canopy formed a constantly shifting pattern on the sidewalk, like water lapping at the tide mark.

Richard and Chaz walked on either side of her, their soft footfalls echoing the sharp retorts made by her heels against the uneven red bricks of the sidewalk. Chaz helped her into the car. A short ride later, Richard pulled up in front of a freestanding white frame house with jaunty magenta trim that likely sent the city mothers into apoplexy when they saw it. Korine couldn't imagine that it had been approved by Savannah's historic association. The trio took the rickety stairs at the rear to the second-floor apartment.

Chaz unlocked the door and ushered the others inside. Now that they were there, and it was time to talk, Korine felt tongue-tied. She looked around curiously at her son's new home. For all the shock value displayed by the exterior of the house, the inside was uncluttered and modern. A pair of mismatched antique tables with clean lines were tucked in next to a violently purple, red, and yellow-print upholstered sofa. Not what Korine had pictured as a typical bachelor's pad. She rather liked it.

The walls were butter yellow. Numerous pieces of equally vivid artwork hung around the room. As Korine browsed the walls, Richard brought a straight-back chair in from the dining room. Peeking through the open door, she could see that it was the only piece of furniture there. Either the couple hadn't gotten around to such formalities before they split up, or Leslie had not left empty-handed. She stopped in front of a picture of a younger Richard. He and another man had their heads together, mugging for the camera.

Chaz's voice was carefully edited as he called to Richard, "Leslie missed one of his pictures."

It took Korine a minute to realize what Chaz had said. Her first thought was that Leslie was a photographer. But Chaz had said "his." Korine's eyes widened in her reflection in the glass over the picture. Leslie was not the photographer, Leslie was the smiling man next to Richard.

As her vision came back into focus, she saw that Chaz's face was also visible. The reflection of both their distorted faces, mother and son, framed the two men smiling behind the glass. She turned and looked silently up at Chaz. He stood there, blue eyes shadowed, brow wrinkled with concentration, trying not to shed the tears that Korine knew were there. He looked much like he had when he'd told her that he was moving back down to Savannah.

As he waited for her reaction, she realized something else. He wasn't concerned about her reaction to his revelation about Richard and Leslie. It cut far deeper than that. This was Chaz's way of telling her his news. Richard had found someone else, and that someone was her son. She felt like she had been slammed against the butter-yellow walls. Drawing a breath in which there wasn't enough oxygen, she looked beyond Chaz to where Richard stood, chair still in his hands. Korine put a shaking hand up to cover her eyes so that she didn't have to look Chaz in the face. She'd wasted so much time. All those someday dreams, cut to ribbons of useless wanting.

Her hand fell away, revealing an anguished son, waiting for her response. The gulf between them stretched. Korine knew she had to say something—say the right thing—before it was too late. She opened her mouth. She shut it again. She couldn't lose Chaz. What if she said the wrong thing? What was the right thing?

"Suppose we sit down," Richard suggested. His cool tone was belied by the fact that he still stood in the center of the room, chair in his hands at waist height.

Korine's ice-cold hand sought her son's. He accepted it gratefully. She went with him to take her place on the opposite end of the surprisingly comfortable couch. She still couldn't find the words to express what she felt. She wasn't sure if she ever would be able to find them. Shock, certainly. Fear of all the things associated with the gay lifestyle. Loss of her own dreams for him. Those were the things Korine found uppermost in her mind. But not one of them was appropriate to say to Chaz at that point in time.

"I've been trying to talk with you all weekend," Chaz said. "But something always comes up, first Leo Gilcrest out on Tybee Beach, then Dodie's death, which deservedly enough took front stage." His tone was bitter, showing how much he had, indeed, minded.

"When did…." Korine's tongue stumbled over the words. "I mean, when did you two…."

"When Leslie moved out and I moved in. This time I knew that their relationship was truly over. So, I finally was able to tell Richard how I felt about him." Chaz turned to Richard and held out his hand in invitation. Richard put down the chair, which he'd still held suspended in midair, sat down upon it next to Chaz, and took the offered hand.

"How did you decide that you were…gay?" Korine forced the proper word to go past her lips. The real questions were those to which she didn't really want to hear the answer: What did I do to make you fear telling me? What did I do to make this happen?

"I didn't *decide* to be gay, I just am. I tried for a long time not to be, but this is the way that God made me. Try as I might, I can't change it. Not even for you." Chaz spoke with a defiant finality, as if he'd anticipated a fight and was prepared with multiple rejoinders.

"I…," Korine began, then felt a tear escape her guard to roll down her cheek. She accepted the handkerchief that Richard handed her, but didn't resort to using it.

"Janey told me that I was going to have to be prepared to let some things go where you were concerned. I guess she was right."

Chaz had a few tears of his own trailing down his cheeks. "I know it's a disappointment to you."

"Of course I'm disappointed," Korine blurted out. When Chaz rose to his feet and turned to go, she realized what she had said. "But not in you!" Korine said, crying now in earnest. "No, this isn't what I would have chosen for any child of mine. But, disappointed *in you?* How could you think that?"

Chaz stood, his back broad and stiff under his polo shirt. Slowly, he turned. "I've been hinting for years."

"Not very hard," Korine responded, feeling a little defensive.

"I told you I wanted to find my own partner. I've talked to you about Richard and Leslie."

"I thought Leslie was a she," Korine said. "You never called him a him!"

Chaz's blue eyes were soft and vulnerable, like a little boy's whose best friend had moved to the moon. "I didn't realize I'd done that."

Richard sat still as stone on his chair. Only his eyes moved as he followed the exchange of words between mother and son.

"Why didn't you tell me before?" Korine asked finally.

"How could I tell you? It means the end of that blasted long line of McFailes in Pine Grove."

"To hell with the succession. We're not a line of kings," Korine said savagely. "I just want you to be happy." She knew that at least a tear or two that fell in the next few seconds were for the grandchildren that she would never have. She had hoped for those. Yet, she would have died rather than lay that burden at Chaz's feet. "I just wish you'd told me sooner."

Korine sat back in the corner of the sofa. Chaz sat down again and said, "That's what Dennis said."

"Dennis knew?" Korine exclaimed. Even her nephew knew?

"He overheard me talking soon after he moved in. I was home for Christmas break and he picked up the extension without my knowing it."

"How could he?" Somehow, Korine had said exactly the right thing.

Chaz broke into a grin for the first time since their conversation had begun. "Listen in?" he said. "He did it all the time. You had no idea what you'd taken on when you brought him under your roof, did you?"

"Evidently not."

For a moment the three of them sat. Against all expectations, the quiet was a friendly one.

Finally, Korine broke the silence. "How long have you known?"

"It's really rather ironic that Richard and Leslie's relationship was the one which helped me to recognize my own preferences. I was always jealous of them." He sent his partner a quick leer, which was taken in good part, and even returned, in Richard's toned-down manner.

"Did you ever talk with your father about this?" Korine asked gently.

"No," Chaz said. "I couldn't. And now, of course, I don't have that luxury."

Richard leaned forward and caught Korine's hands in his. "Thank you," he said.

Korine pulled back before she could think. Richard felt her resistance to his touch and let go. "For what?" she asked, trying to cover her gaff.

"For accepting your son," Richard said formally. "My mother still won't speak to me."

Korine stood and bent over to hug Richard. Reaching out with one hand, she gathered in Chaz as well. It wasn't the extended family she had envisioned, but if Chaz was going to be happy with Richard, so would she. In time, anyway, she thought as she looked at Richard's rugged profile. In time.

THE MEN DROVE HER back to the hotel. It wasn't until she had her key card out ready to unlock her door that she realized she hadn't spoken to Chaz at all about her own secret. Korine's mouth formed a word that her own mother would never have let cross her lips. She realized with a start that she stood in the hall in front of her door, one hand cradling her stomach as she'd seen Janey do countless times since her miscarriage.

Savagely, Korine opened the door to find that someone had slipped a folded sheet of paper under her door while she was out. Recognizing J.J.'s cramped handwriting on the outside of the note, she threw it on the table next to her bed.

She could figure out what it said without reading it.

J.J. wanted to know why she was acting so odd about Leo Gilcrest. He would simply have to wait his turn. She had two other men she needed to talk with on that subject before J.J. got the tale.

FIFTEEN

J.J. BRACED ONE HAND ON the door, holding his weight. The other beat a steady tattoo on Korine's door. Janey had gone out for breakfast with a few ladies from the now-defunct conference, which left him free to try and pry at a few loose ends in the hope that they'd unravel something promising.

He'd slipped a note under Korine's door about midnight the night before. As J.J. had expected, she hadn't called him. Raising his hand to knock again, he hoped he'd gotten there in plenty of time to catch her before she went out.

Korine opened the door a crack. J.J.'s foot shot forward into the narrow opening. "J.J., this isn't a good time," she said.

Not relaxing his stance, he continued to press forward until the bulk of his body stood firmly in the doorway proper so that she couldn't even try to shut the door. He didn't say anything, just looked at her reproachfully.

Korine stood aside. "Don't do that!"

"I'm not the one holding out—again," J.J. said as he went past her.

"J.J., I'm not holding out on you, I swear."

"You may have to," J.J. replied. "Swear, that is." He stood before her doodles in the condensation on the window. He traced one set of initials that hung there like damning carvings on an old tree trunk: L.G. K.McF. No heart. He turned and spoke seriously. "Did Leo find you yesterday?"

"No. I went out to dinner with Chaz soon after Janey left here. I didn't run into anyone."

"Are you ready to face him?"

Korine looked lightheaded. "Face him?"

"Leo's pretty darn determined to talk with you privately. You ready for that?"

Her smile lines flashed briefly, although what she found funny about all this was beyond him. "I think so. After last night, there isn't anything that Leo can throw at me that will faze me."

"Last night?" J.J. asked.

"Dinner with Chaz and his partner, Richard." Korine put an extra flourish on the word *partner*.

"Well, congratulations!" J.J. said. "I didn't know that Chaz had made partner already."

Korine sat down in the chair and threw back her head and laughed. "I wasn't talking law, J.J. Sit down. I need to tell you a story."

Five minutes later, J.J. was speechless. He suspected that the news affected Korine more than she was letting on. Evidently, Chaz had left it to his mother to break the news to her friends. No wonder she wasn't worried about Leo Gilcrest any longer.

J.J. pulled himself back together. "So, when are you

going to explain this to me?" He pointed back over his shoulder at the telltale doodling on the window.

"Childish, isn't it? Reliving those dreams of youth. I can't tell you why Leo's so pestering now, because he most certainly wasn't that way when I knew him."

J.J. shook his finger at Korine. Even though she was older than he by almost a decade, he sometimes felt like her parent. "As far as I'm concerned, you're sitting on the clue that could lead us to find out who killed Dodie. It's not up to you what you hold back and what you tell."

"Us?"

"Sudley finally decided he couldn't do this without me," J.J. said lightly.

Korine saw right through that one. "Couldn't keep your nose out of it, could you?"

"I've told you this before. Withholding evidence can allow a guilty person to go free."

"I know that." Korine looked miserable, as she should. "Listen, I know you don't believe me, but what happened to us didn't have anything to do with Dodie. And I'd like to talk with both Leo and Chaz before I can talk with you."

"Today," J.J. pressed.

"I promise." Feeling childish, Korine did the whole cross-my-heart-and-hope-to-die pantomime. "Chaz is supposed to come over this morning before work. I'll talk to Leo before noon. Then I'll talk to you. Now go on. I'm sure you've got other things to check out."

He hauled himself out of the comfortable chair and went to the door. "I'll bring you lunch."

"We'll talk then," Korine agreed as she shut the door behind him.

J.J. returned downstairs to his room. Opening the door, he was greeted by the lingering humidity from Janey's shower. He sniffed appreciatively. The smell of Suave shampoo and baby powder still lay in the air. A flurry of discarded nightclothes on the bed told of a rushed departure. She must have been late for breakfast.

Shoving everything over to make room to sit on the bed, J.J. picked up the phone. Fifteen minutes later, he got up and put his shoes back on. The county clerk where Fiona Gilcrest had died was going to fax him the death certificate. He'd pick it up in a little while.

He still hadn't gotten over to the hospital to see Sharon, and Holly's defense of her mother notwith-standing-and despite the poisoning—the woman was still a candidate in his mind. He had quite a few questions to put to Dodie's cousin.

J.J. had called the hospital, and the operator cautiously confirmed Sharon was still a patient but declined to give out any information on which floor she was being treated. J.J. knew by the weary sound of the operator's voice that she must have already received a lot of calls that morning on the same subject. Press probably. Two poisonings in one weekend would generate a lot of interest. He tucked his pad and pen into a pocket and headed downstairs.

J.J. STOPPED FIRST in the hospital gift shop to buy a plant for Sharon, his excuse to get into the room. Holly was hiding behind a pair of ridiculous sunglasses in front of the counter, her weight resting on one foot, while she paid for a Diet Coke and cheese crackers. He resisted saying "Boo." When she turned around and found him standing behind her, she jumped anyway. J.J. was used to people looking at him like he was a wall they'd like to dynamite to get out of their way. It had never touched him the way it did now.

The girl's eyes had smudges under them from lack of sleep, visible even through the dark lenses of the movie-star frames which covered half her face. Holly looked utterly tired. And utterly defeated. She was even too exhausted to spit words at him the way she had the day before. "Go away," she said.

J.J. wondered if anyone said that to Sudley. He certainly didn't hear it when he had his uniform on at home. "How is your mom doing this morning?" he asked gently.

"I don't have to talk to you," Holly said. Some of the fire that had lit her attitude the day before returned.

"No," J.J. replied. "You don't. But Janey's going to be mighty disappointed with me if I don't bring back a full report. And I've got to confess, I'd like to talk to you—pick your brain a little bit about Dodie—before I go see your mom. Sudley's that close to an arrest, and I'd hate for him to get the wrong person." J.J. hated being deceitful with people, but he wasn't really lying, just like he wasn't really investigating. He simply needed to ask, simply needed to know that the guilty party was going to be punished. Janey had called it a compulsion the night before. She wasn't far off in her estimate.

"Fine," Holly said, flipping her hair back over her shoulder and standing as tall as her five-foot-five frame would allow. J.J. still towered over her. She turned and led the way to some faded chairs in the hospital lobby.

She settled sulkily into one of the chairs and tore into the crackers with her teeth. Huddled into the chair, hair still damp and tousled from the shower, she looked like a sparrow fluffed up against a cold wind. That J.J. was the cold wind who had caused all her protective ruffling was a given. He knew that she expected no good to come from him. She might even be right.

J.J. sat on the couch, the closest seat to Holly's, and let her eat a few crackers in peace. Once she'd popped the top of the soda can and swallowed enough caffeine so that she might be up to answering questions, he decided to begin.

"Your mom's doing better?" J.J. prompted.

"Yes, a bit," Holly answered grudgingly.

"Can you tell me who you saw on Saturday morning? When and where?"

"And this is going to keep Sudley from arresting Mom?"

J.J. didn't correct this leap of logic. He just looked encouraging and waited.

Holly eyed him uncertainly, then began. "I was helping Mom, running all the hell over the place looking for missing recording equipment, missing speakers, missing paperwork, missing coffee cups. And no, I didn't kill Dodie in the middle of all that. I didn't have time, among other things."

"Can you give me some idea who you ran into and in what order?"

"Janey. Your wife," Holly added unnecessarily. "In the hallway outside the conference rooms. Looking for you." She continued in a singsong voice, "I saw Korine go into the conference room to hear the rosarian. I was looking for the technician who was supposed to have been there early to make sure that we had copies of the tape from that session to sell later. He never did show. Then I went upstairs to talk to Javier—at the front desk—about paging Linda, the conference liaison, to get some coffee cups to go with the coffee, creamer, and sugar they'd delivered. Leo was up there at the same time. He asked me where Dodie was."

"And when did you see your mother?" J.J. prompted when Holly stopped abruptly.

"Mom? In between everything else. She was like a madwoman trying to keep everything together. Leo was supposed to be helping, but between Dodie and Korine, he wasn't all that into plants this weekend."

"So your mother resented that?"

"Sure she did," Holly replied. She removed the sunglasses and tossed them on the table, the better to be able to level a glare at J.J. "Wouldn't you?"

"Your mom worked very hard to make this weekend a success, didn't she?"

"She most certainly did! Dodie's death would have been hard enough, but coming now—ruining all the work she did—it's totally devastated her. Then the detective came over to the house and accused her of killing her own cousin. As if she would."

J.J. regarded Holly. He didn't think she realized how much she'd given away about Sharon's priorities. "Your father was there when Sudley talked with Sharon, wasn't he?"

"That's another thing," Holly said, sitting up straight and glaring once again at J.J. "You went and got Dad all stirred up, just after Mom had him calmed down again."

"You know, I have trouble seeing your dad stirred up about anything. Remarkably calm man."

"Shows what you know." Holly drained her soda and plunked the can down on the glass-topped table in front of her. Tucking her feet under her, she looked even more like a small bedraggled bird as she sat there. She bit her lip and looked away.

If Korine wasn't acting so strange, J.J. would have liked to try to get her to talk with Holly. Korine and Janey were both better with people than he was. He realized the direction his thoughts were going and shut that down immediately. No way was he going to get Korine and Janey involved in this.

J.J. said gently, "I know how tough this is for you."

"Do you?" Holly asked bluntly. "Do you have any idea? At first, I thought the police would do their job and catch the murderer. But now, they're not even looking at anyone but Mom."

"I'm pretty sure that's not true." J.J. decided that might be a good segue into Leo's involvement with Dodie. "How long ago were Dodie and Leo Gilcrest dating?"

"Way before I remember, but she always talked about him. I think they worked together at a florist shop when they were young. He lived down the street from us, so she always saw him when she came to visit." Holly's bruised blue eyes sought his. "Do you think he killed her?"

"I don't know yet who killed her. How about you? Who do you think killed your cousin?"

"I don't know," Holly said. The girl shivered.

"If I asked your mother, who would she say killed Dodie?" J.J. asked softly.

"You don't want to see how Mom is, you're just trying to hurt us!" Just that fast, the frightened bird had turned into a hissing, spitting hellcat. Holly sprang from her chair and stood there, fists balled and ready to fight. "Stay away from my mom! She's had enough!"

Her timing could not have been better. Winslow chose that moment to walk in the front door. As soon as he saw J.J. with Holly, her father came striding over. The man wouldn't have been particularly glad to see J.J. in the first place, but under the circumstances, he was livid. "What's going on here?" he demanded.

"Holly and I were talking about how much we both want whoever killed Dodie to be caught and punished for the crime," J.J. answered in a level tone.

"Dodie isn't worth crying over," Winslow said, giving his daughter a disdainful look. "Come along, your mother will be waiting."

Holly hung back. Obviously, she wasn't kidding when she had mocked J.J.'s observation that Winslow had good self-control. The girl looked even more terrified of her father than she had been of J.J.

"You are so much like your mother," Winslow said in a slow, painstaking voice. It was not a compliment. Holly shrank inside her sweatshirt. The man turned to J.J. "As for you, I'm swearing out a complaint of harassment against you as soon as I get to a phone."

"There's one over there on the wall." J.J. couldn't resist pushing a little to see what the man would do.

Winslow turned to face J.J. and looked him up and down and said, "I thought you said that you weren't with the Savannah police."

"I'm not. But a police officer is a police officer, even when he's off his home ground. Crime is attractive to me, Mr. Winslow. I like to find out who committed them and make sure they see justice meted out in full."

The two men stared at each other for a full minute. J.J. smiled slightly as Winslow blinked. His eyes, when they broke the contact, sought his daughter's form as she stood by his side. "Go on up to your mother," he ordered. Holly went.

J.J. regarded Winslow. "Can I ask you about Leo Gilcrest and his relationship with Dodie? Are you willing to talk about that?"

Winslow nodded his head regally, covering the fact that he was capitulating. "No one in the family had the slightest reason to do Dodie any harm. Leo and That Woman are another matter."

J.J. forbore reminding Winslow that That Woman was one of his best friends, and he took his seat again.

Winslow took the other chair and began, "Leo Gilcrest and Dodie were supposed to get married a little over twenty years ago. She lived with us then. She'd moved in to help Sharon after one of her miscarriages, and never seemed to move on." He shook his head and plowed on with his tale. "Anyway, Dodie came home one night without his ring. Wouldn't tell us anything, just went into her room and wouldn't come out for days." He continued, "Sharon tried, I tried. She wouldn't talk to either of us."

"Holly said he lived close to you now," J.J. said.

"Down the street. He moved there just before his wife died."

"I'm sorry," J.J. apologized. "When did you say that Leo and Dodie took up their relationship again?"

"They didn't," Winslow said.

"Sharon's been accusing Korine on the strength of the impression that Dodie and Leo were involved again."

"Sharon believed a lot of things that Dodie told her, most of which weren't true. Dodie almost broke up our marriage before Holly came along, saying that I had made advances toward her. It took me a while, but Sharon finally saw that it was the other way around." Winslow's expression showed clearly how painful he found that revelation to be.

"Korine got the impression that there was mutual interest between Dodie and Leo," J.J. offered.

Winslow stirred in his chair. "Leo wanted a fun weekend. It's about the only thing you do with a woman like Dodie."

J.J. honored Winslow with a slight smile. At least someone was being honest about the victim. "It's interesting that Gilcrest moved down the street from you."

"Actually, it's been fine. At first, we were worried that Dodie's frequent visits would make it uncomfortable. But she soon moved up to the mountains, so it was only awkward when Dodie came to see us."

"Which was fairly often," J.J. said.

Winslow regarded him. "Yes. Dodie and Sharon are—were—close."

J.J. didn't answer. His subconscious was telling him something. He wished like hell that he knew what it was.

He looked at his watch and discovered that it was time for him to meet Korine. Entrusting the plant for Sharon to Winslow, J.J. gave the startled man a hasty thanks. He left the hospital to find his car. Korine had proven to be very slippery to pin down lately. Sharon wasn't going anywhere. He'd be back.

SIXTEEN

CHAZ AND RICHARD waited in the other room. They'd been early, and Korine had been about to step in the shower when they'd let themselves in. Leaving them to enjoy a cup of coffee while they consumed the pastries they'd brought, she'd promised to hurry.

Toweling her hair dry, Korine allowed herself the luxury of remembering the handsome boy that Leo Gilcrest had been when he went by the nickname "Mick." She wasn't sure how Chaz would take it when she told him the full story. It wasn't like she was asking him to accept a new family member into his life. It had been more than thirty years since Leo had declared his undying love for her, then walked off, never to be heard from again. Korine frowned and tossed the damp towel on the counter. Why skip all those years in between and pick up here and now?

She wrapped a dry terry bath sheet around herself and made a face at the mirror. Leo's love may have been undying, but communicative it was not. There had been ample opportunity to contact her all these years. She'd lived in the same little bungalow on the coast for two full years after he'd left town. Even after she'd married Charlie, she wasn't exactly lost for good. Her mother still lived in that house.

Almost as if thinking about Madeira Stewart's home conjured up a sea breeze, a draft skittered around her ankles. Startled, she looked toward the door. Someone was moving across the carpeting in her room.

"Chaz?" she called out.

The motion stopped.

Korine stood still on the terrazzo floor, a statue in white terry, wondering what the heck to do. Whoever was out there stood between her and her clothes.

A man cleared his throat. "Um," his voice unimaginatively said.

Korine relaxed. No one who intended to do her harm would sound that uncertain. One hand holding the towel firmly in place, she poked her head around the door.

Leo Gilcrest stood rooted in the center of her room, a white grocery bag dangling from one hand. "Your son let me in. He said he had to go downstairs to take care of something for a minute, then he'd be back. Your lawyer went with him."

Korine regarded Leo. She could still see traces of the earnest young man he had been. The spot on his neck that the razor had missed that morning. The way his Adam's apple bobbed after he spoke.

Leo took her silence for anger. "The policeman dropped this off. I'll just leave it here and go."

"Throw it on the bed, then wait in the other room. We have a few things to talk about." Korine spoke gently. It would, after all, serve no useful purpose if she took her once-upon-a-time battered emotions out on him now.

Leo deposited the bag and left, closing the door behind him. She waited a second, then went across and locked the door. Turning to the bag, she divested it of its contents. Her missing toothbrush and toothpaste. Turning to the closet, Korine pulled out her pink blouse and floral skirt. Shaking them out, she eyed the wrinkles critically. They'd have to do for a reunion.

Five minutes later, having applied makeup like armor, she unlocked the door and walked out into the main room.

The two of them were alone. Chaz and Richard were still missing. Just as well. She'd rather tackle this one male at a time. Exchanging small talk about the weather like wampum, Leo and Korine eased into the chairs. Korine caught her hand rubbing the nap of the chair again. She wondered if, before she was allowed to go home, she would have worn it completely away.

She folded her hands together in her lap like a good little girl. Forcing herself to look Leo in the face, she asked, "So, where have you been half my life?" She hadn't intended it to come out so abruptly.

Leo flushed. "I wrote you. You never responded."

"You wrote? I never got anything from you. I didn't even know you'd left town. Suddenly, your phone line was disconnected. Nothing. Zip. Nada." So much for not inflicting her lacerated feelings on him.

"I stopped by the day I left and asked your mom to give you my letter. I guess she decided that, after that one date, we didn't need to stay in touch. She wasn't exactly thrilled with me to begin with, you know."

Her mom had protested when Korine told her she was seeing Mick McGilley that night. Korine's stomach squirmed with an equal mixture of resentment and embarrassment. Madeira, who was usually so openhearted, might have thought she was protecting her daughter. "What did the letter say?" Korine asked.

"Nothing specific," Leo answered. "Just cut my heart out and pasted it on the page."

Korine gave that melodramatic statement the consideration it deserved. Then, for a minute, she was back in the small bedroom on the second floor she'd shared with her older sister. For weeks after Leo had gone, she tried to follow Kindra's advice and forget all about him. Remembered all the nights her mother had tiptoed in and comforted the sleepless girls. Kindra and Korine had been drinking that night, as well as the boys. The wreck wasn't really the fault of any one of the four. Nate had continued to drink long after the rest of them had tried to stop him. When Leo wrestled the keys away from Nate, he'd made the decision to hand them to Korine since she was the soberest of the bunch. Just not sober enough to see the truck as she pulled out onto the highway.

"Mother never told me."

"I figured as much." Leo paused. Then, dropping his weight forward, he rested his elbows on his knees. He held his hands out parallel to the ground and examined the backs closely, as if the wrinkles he'd gained since they last met would give him a road map of what to say. "When you didn't recognize me, I was pretty sure you'd forgotten all about me. Or blamed me like everyone else."

Korine made a small sound of negation.

Leo looked up, shoulders hunched, hands clasped between his knees. "It's too late, isn't it?"

"Too late for what, Leo?" Now it was Korine's turn to lean forward. "For whatever reason, you left town and my mother decided that it would be less painful if I thought you'd simply disappeared." She looked across the space between them. It seemed insurmountable. "Why didn't you just tell me who you were the other night?"

"In front of Dodie?" Leo looked across the three-foot gap between them as if it were an abyss.

Korine sat back. "And it mattered what Dodie thought?"

"No. Yes," Leo said, his voice husky. "I didn't think saying, 'Hello Korine, I'm that guy who got drunk with you down on the dunes a long time ago. The one who was with you when your sister's fiancé was killed. Long time, no see,' would go over too well right then."

Her face flamed. He might as well have slapped her.

"You never wrote back," he said. "For all I knew, you felt the same way about me that your mom did."

"I wouldn't have gone out with you if I had! Much less—" Korine stopped. She was shaking. Feeling much like that teenaged mass of nerves that had eventually scabbed over—no longer bleeding, but still painful— Korine held a silent debate with herself.

"What?" Leo asked. His intense look raked her face.

They'd known each other for such a short time, but she felt as naked with him emotionally as she had with Charlie.

"We'd all had way too much to drink," she said. "None of us had any business driving. In many ways we were all guilty in Nate's death. It wasn't your fault that you were the one whose dad would buy him the stuff." Korine had to stop to grab a tissue from the box next to her.

"What the...." Comprehension dawned on Leo's face. "You blame me?"

"Kindra told Nate's mom that you'd bought the beer," Korine tried to explain. "That, on top of you supposedly driving, made everything much worse. It was horrible."

"It was more horrible for me. A few years later I got into another scrape, and they threw me into a correctional facility because of my record."

Korine looked across that gulf between them, at the stricken man sitting there. She made a decision. She stood and went over and knelt in front of Leo. Gathering his large rough hands in her own, she looked up at him. "I'm so sorry that we let you be blamed."

Leo tore his hands away. "I'm sorry too, Korine. I had some notion of flirting with you this weekend, making you remember me. I needed to know why you never wrote back. It never occurred to me that you'd blamed me for Nate's death."

"I didn't blame you. My sister didn't either, not really. Kindra told folks that you were at fault so that Nate's memory could go on." Korine focused her gaze on the paisley pattern in the wallpaper behind Leo's head. Anything rather than face the betrayal in his eyes. "So where does Dodie fit into all this? Was she part of getting back at me for not responding to your letters?" She made herself look at him.

"No!" Leo's answer exploded from his throat. "I wasn't looking for revenge. I ran across your picture in an old magazine my wife had in the potting shed several years ago. I was clearing it out after her death. I even called once. When you answered…I couldn't speak, so I hung up. Then I heard you'd be here this weekend. It was like we were being pushed together. I just wanted to see…."

"See what?" Korine prompted when he stopped.

"See how you'd turned out. See if you still had that softness to you." His voice cut across her nerves like sandpaper.

"What did you have in mind, a one-night stand to get me back for all those years ago?" The pattern on the wall began to swim across her vision.

Leo pulled Korine to her feet. His hands dug into her elbows as he shook her hard once, then let her go. "No, dammit!" he said roughly. He placed his hands softly on either side of her face and cupped it, looking straight into her eyes. "I can still see that kindness of spirit in your eyes. I needed to meet you back then. I'd never seen anyone like you. Caring, not grabbing every little thing I had, not looking to take, but to give. I had no idea that people could be like that. Your mother was right about one thing," Leo went on dryly. "The McGilleys weren't from the right side of the tracks in many, many ways."

"And what we did was right?" Korine's mouth tasted of ashes. "Good intentions doesn't provide an excuse for our actions."

"No, it doesn't. But what are we going to do about that now?"

"Dodie—"

"To hell with Dodie! We dated for a while back when we were kids. For crying out loud, that was almost as long ago as you and me. But I can assure you that I never tried to keep up with Dodie the way I wanted to with you."

"I'm not talking about being jealous," Korine said, although his words were reassuring. "I'm talking about a motive for killing her. I can assure you that once Sudley knows what happened to us way back when, he's going to assume that one or the other—or both of us—did her in."

Leo's face grew red. "How many times—" he bit off the words like they were too hot to string together "—do I have to tell you...."

"It's not me," Korine said, a little too loudly. "It's Sudley! He thinks he's got us tied up in pretty little packages. Right now he's confused. For all we know, Sharon sent those chocolates to herself. But yesterday, he believed what Sharon was saying about me. Sharon's parroting Dodie. No matter what you say, Dodie's words weigh more heavily in the balance for the police than yours do."

"Do you think I killed her?" he asked.

Korine looked at him. "As you said to Sudley, there's been a whole lot of water under the bridge since we knew each other. That first date wasn't the first time we'd spent hours together. All that talking after school, accidental meetings at the Dairy Queen. We weren't strangers." Even now, having him that close was robbing her of the breath she needed to finish what she had to say. "I don't think the boy I knew back then could kill in cold blood. But I don't know you anymore. Neither," she added, "do you know me."

"I see," was all Leo said. He took a step backward and turned on his heel. Walking to the door, he ignored Korine's protests and opened it. Shaking her hand off his arm, he walked out and slammed the door.

Korine laid her head against the door. It wouldn't do her any good to go running down the hall after him. After all those years of waiting to deal with him, Leo would wait a little while longer. Her son would be back shortly and she would need to deal with his reaction to her story about the death so long ago of her sister's fiancé.

Pressing the palms of her hands to her eyes, she wiped away the tears. Korine had known it would be hard to face this. She'd known how difficult it would be for Leo to find that they'd let him take the entire blame for what they had all done. After all, it had gone against everything that Korine held dear to allow Kindra and their mother to talk her into the story that they ultimately told the public. Over the years, Korine thought that she had atoned somewhat for that sin. She hadn't realized how deeply that meeting would rip her own scars apart.

SEVENTEEN

KORINE ANSWERED right away when J.J. called from the pay phone by the gift shop. He had decided to call before driving all the way back to the hotel.

"I'm fine," Korine said, although J.J. could tell by the sound of her voice that she wasn't. "Leo just left."

"Good. Don't let him back in the door."

"I don't think he'll be back," she said. "Besides, I think you're wrong about him."

J.J. heard knocking in the background. Korine put the phone down and he could hear muffled talking.

Korine fumbled the phone when she returned, and J.J. jumped as the receiver struck the table. "Someone's here," she said breathlessly. "I'd better let you go." Without waiting to hear his reply, she hung up.

J.J. swore. An older woman passing him by shook her head at him. He forced himself to stop and think before he ran out to the car and drove back to the hotel like a crazy person. He fished in his pocket and pulled out thirty-five cents. The quarter was one of the new state ones. He shoved it in the slot anyway. It was a crazy idea, anyhow, to save one of the quarters from every state he visited while he was there. The hotel operator connected him with his room. No answer. He left a message.

He shoved more coins in and tried Korine's room. No answer. J.J. told himself it was probably only Chaz. He was still telling himself that as he headed out to the parking lot.

Casting a covetous glance back at the hospital through his rearview mirror, J.J.'s fury grew. Damn Korine anyhow. Damn himself, while he was at it. He should have made Korine talk to him that morning. He had questions he wanted to ask Sharon. Questions about what Leo Gilcrest had lost that he thought Sharon knew all about. Questions about who had really put that poison in those chocolates. Dodie might have had them delivered, but he didn't think for one minute that Dodie had poisoned them.

Entering the hotel by the side door, J.J. took the elevator to Korine's room. Barreling down the hallway, he pounded on her door. No answer. He banged again. Desperate now, he shouted her name. He heard the elevator behind him ding as the door opened. Korine, looking disheveled but very much alive, peered out at him.

"Where were you? Are you all right?" J.J. fired questions at Korine as he backed her into the room.

A man's voice from behind him in the hallway said, "Is there a problem here, ma'am?"

"No," Korine and J.J. said at the same time.

"Shall I call security?" the man asked, looking steadily at Korine. He was half the size of J.J., yet he looked as though he'd defend her to the death.

"It's fine," Korine said more steadily. "Really," she added. "Come on in," she said to J.J.

The man backed away, looking like he regretted offering his assistance. He slid his key into his own door and entered the room, shaking his head.

Korine shut her door. Leo Gilcrest stood by the window.

J.J. turned an angry gaze on Korine. She shrugged and said, "I told you he wasn't going to hurt me. We've been catching up."

"When did your wife die?" J.J. asked.

"What?" Leo said.

"Your wife died within two weeks of Charlie McFaile. How convenient was that?"

"J.J., Charlie died of cancer. Leo's wife died in a car wreck. Does it matter when that happened?" Korine asked.

"It does if he had to lie about it."

"I didn't lie."

J.J. glared at Leo.

"All right. I did lie to you. It took me years to get up the nerve to try and reach Korine. I didn't think she would want to see me."

J.J. started to speak, but Korine interrupted. "That's enough!" she said. "I know you think he had something to do with Dodie's death and that he might do something to harm me; but as I told you, that won't happen."

J.J. opened his mouth again but was interrupted this time by Leo. "I told you before that I liked you better for the loyalty you showed to Korine. Enough is enough. I didn't hurt Dodie, and I won't hurt Korine."

"What was it that Dodie took from you that you wanted more than anything else in the world?"

Leo took a step forward. "How did you know about that?"

"Sharon isn't as likely to protect you, once she thinks she's been poisoned."

For some reason, that seemed to reassure Leo. "Sharon is the last person to tell you about that," he replied. Turning to Korine, he said, "The thing that I wanted most in the world was a child. Dodie stole that from me."

"Holly," J.J. guessed.

Leo arched his eyebrows. "Very good. How did you know?"

"Let's just say that I have a little bit of experience with illegitimate children from past cases."

His statement had the desired effect on Korine, who had been getting more and more withdrawn. She smiled slightly and regained color. "Holly is your child?" she asked.

"According to Dodie, she is. She resembles my mother's family. Sharon's reaction when I told her I knew Dodie had given my child up for adoption supports it." Leo turned to J.J. "Which is why I'm so sure that Sharon didn't talk to you. But," he added politely, "I am at your service."

"But why did Dodie give her up?" Korine asked.

"After we'd been together for about six months, I decided that Dodie wasn't the woman I was looking for, and we drifted apart. I ran into her many years later, and she looked a whole lot better to me than she had when we split up. About a month after we started dating again, Dodie let slip that she'd given up a baby for adoption. From the timing, I assumed she was mine. Dodie later confirmed that."

"Does Holly know she's Dodie's daughter?" Korine asked.

Leo said, "Dodie was sorry she told me from the minute she opened her mouth. As long as I'm doing true confessions, I might as well tell you that Sharon is telling the truth about one thing: Dodie had good reason to think we might be getting friendlier." Leo had the grace to look ashamed. "I was using her. I didn't want to look a fool if Korine recognized me and treated me badly."

Leo pulled out his wallet and took out a hundred dollar bill. He must have saved it when J.J. refused it earlier. Holding it out in front of him, he said to J.J., "If Dodie told Sharon that we were getting back together, she might also have said she wanted Holly to know who her real parents were. I still think that Sharon killed Dodie to keep Holly."

Ignoring the money in Leo's outstretched hand, J.J. picked up the phone and dialed Sudley's office. He held up one hand to forestall Korine's objections. "If she's guilty—and I'm not convinced yet—and if he'd told Sudley this choice bit of news yesterday, then Sharon should be behind bars now and not resting comfortably in the hospital, thinking that this latest ruse will have confused everyone all to hell.

"Which it did," he said as Sudley picked up the phone.

"Bascom?" Sudley inquired. "Which what did what?"

J.J. handed the phone to Leo. "Talk to the man."

As J.J. listened, Leo repeated, nearly word for word, what he'd just revealed to the two of them. When Leo was finished, he handed the phone back.

"Wait," J.J. told Sudley. Even though he hadn't yet managed to pry the story of her past relationship with Leo Gilcrest out of Korine, he knew that she would eventually have to tell Sudley anyway. She might as well tell them both at the same time. "There's more." And he handed the phone to Korine.

Ignoring her pleading look, he walked over and obliterated the barely visible initials on the window. As he listened, J.J. felt pain gnaw at his gut. He had known that Leo and Korine's past relationship had been a factor in her current behavior. He hadn't realized how bad the experience had been. It was a horrible episode, and they'd done the wrong thing. Judging from the pain in Korine's voice as she recited the bare details of a first date gone incredibly wrong, she'd paid the price for her mistake every day since.

As much as he wanted to be able to give her a smile of encouragement, J.J. forced himself to wait until she hung up before he turned around. She had to learn not to withhold evidence, no matter how personally painful or embarrassing it might be.

"He said to tell you he'd look up Holly's birth certificate and to say thank you." Korine looked as miserable as she sounded.

"Does Chaz know about this?" J.J. asked.

"No," Korine replied. "He hasn't gotten here yet."

"You'd better call him now. You may have to tell him over the phone," Leo said gently. "If you don't, someone will call Richard and tell him. And then he'll be the one to break the news to your son."

Korine and Leo stood there, mere feet apart, but separated by a lot of history. Both of their faces showed traces of wonder, affection, and hesitant forgiveness, the three ingredients for renewed love. J.J. took a good look at Leo Gilcrest and, despite continued reservations about him, didn't see that Korine was in any danger. The two of them had a lot to talk about. He turned and left. J.J. suspected that they didn't even see him go.

JAVIER WAS STILL at the desk when J.J. got back downstairs. "Saturday morning. You were working, weren't you?" J.J. asked.

"Yes," the young man replied, his Savannah drawl made deeper by his caution in answering.

"So who was around that morning?"

"Everyone, sir."

"Specifically, Mrs. Winslow and her daughter?"

"They were both here. Mrs. Winslow several times." Javier's rugged face grew animated as he remembered the day. "I don't remember times though. Think you could get Holly's phone number for me?" Javier paused hopefully. "No?" He swallowed regretfully. "I know what time she was around. She came up around ten-thirty and wanted the hotel liaison."

"Ten-thirty?"

"I'm pretty sure because it was after my break."

"What about Mr. Gilcrest?"

"Gilcrest," Javier said. "Him, I don't like. Can you arrest him for it?"

"If he did it," J.J. answered shortly. He still wondered if he'd done the right thing by leaving Korine and Leo alone. "When did you see him?"

"Before my break. He came up looking for Mrs. Winslow."

"And when did you see him again?"

"After my break. He came down the elevator and talked to Mrs. Winslow and Holly a few minutes. Your wife came over and talked to them too, then he went downstairs."

J.J. thought a minute. "Did you happen to notice if any of them changed their clothes?"

"No." Javier's voice held more than a note of regret.

"Okay. Thanks," J.J. said, intending to go catch up with Janey.

"Let me know when you find out who did it." Javier's voice followed J.J. hopefully.

J.J. turned around and sketched a salute to the young man. It was better than anything else he could have done. Javier's face creased in a smile.

J.J. crossed the lobby and picked up the house phone. Janey picked up on the second ring.

"Hey," J.J. said.

"Where have you been?" she exclaimed. "I have looked every which where I could think of to look and you're not there."

"Don't tell me that your thermometer says it's time again. It can't be. I've got things to do."

"I need to talk to you," Janey said.

"You had lunch?" J.J. asked.

"I'll be right down."

Five minutes later Janey walked off the elevator and joined her husband in the restaurant. "Have you seen Korine today?" she asked.

"As a matter of fact—"

"Well, is she all right?" Janey asked. "I talked to her a little while ago. She said she wasn't up to seeing anyone. Why?"

"She and Leo are up there talking right now. I think she'll want to talk to you herself on that one, honey."

Janey gave him an unreadable look before dipping her head. Circling the rim of the glass with her forefinger, she asked, "Did Korine finally talk to Chaz?"

J.J. involuntarily spit the mouthful of tea he'd just sipped back into the glass. "Are you a witch, woman? I was going to wait and let Korine tell you about Chaz. How'd you find out?"

"It wasn't hard. He'll be much happier now that she knows."

"Yeah, but will *she?*"

"Eventually. I hope she took it well. Those two are far too important to each other." Janey pushed her finger around a few more times, then took another sip of her tea.

"Out with it," J.J. said.

Janey looked startled. "What?"

"What's on your mind?"

"Now you're the one casting spells and reading minds." Janey inspected the palm of one hand carefully, running her forefinger, damp from the cold glass, down her lifeline and back up again. "Korine talks to you. She doesn't talk to me that way."

"You upset that she didn't call you right away about Chaz?"

"I suppose." Janey sighed and shook her hand in the air as if warding off evil thoughts.

"I think Korine feels about you like she does Dennis and Katie Anne. She's adopted you. Korine will have to mother you a while before she turns to you as a friend. Confidences and so forth may come with time, but I don't know if she'll ever talk to you the way she does to Amilou."

"And to you."

Janey's words hung in the air like an accusation.

"You jealous of Korine?" J.J. asked carefully.

Janey forced a laugh. "Actually, I think I'm jealous of you."

J.J. sat back and regarded his wife. Slowly, he said, "I can't do anything about how Korine feels about me. I don't think that she will talk to you any more or any less if she and I grow apart."

"I know that." Janey looked miserable. She took a sip of her tea and made a face. "It's bitter."

"Are you talking about the tea, or the way life unfolds?" He lowered his voice. "I understand how you feel. But, how are we going to deal with this when a small person comes into our house? Is our child going to come between us? Are we going to always wonder who he or she loves the most?"

Janey flinched. "I don't know." She looked up from the seemingly fascinating spot on the table in front of her. "I can't believe I finally told you that."

"You know, my grandmother always said that as long as she and Granddaddy could talk, things were okay. Now, their notion of talking, and ours, are pretty far apart. Gran had quite a temper." J.J. smiled as he remembered one flying frying pan that had missed his startled grandfather's nose by inches. "But she had the gist of it right."

"We can talk, can't we?" Janey asked.

J.J. reached out and hauled her chair over next to his. Putting one arm around her, he said, "Didn't I ask you to tell me what was on your mind? Didn't I listen?"

"Yes," Janey said. Her voice was breathless. Her face barely a foot away from his, J.J. could see her nostrils flare as she breathed him in. "And you're not mad," she said with wonder.

J.J. shook his head and smiled tenderly back down at her. "Not mad." He kissed her gently. "But hungry as hell. Let's order."

They opened the menus.

EIGHTEEN

"I CAN'T JUST SIT in the hotel and wait for Sudley to figure out everything." J.J. paced their room. After they'd finished lunch, Janey had talked him into some sightseeing time. She had particularly wanted to visit the First African Baptist Church. Reportedly the first church in America for African-Americans, it had a museum attached that was worth getting by to see. The concierge at the hotel told them that as long as they got there before three-thirty, it would probably be open. Janey had dragged J.J. out into the sunshine, tucked his hand firmly in hers, and walked him the length of the downtown district.

J.J. did have to admit that the walk had done him good. He'd enjoyed the museum too. The man who'd let them in was welcoming and informative. Even so, it wasn't long before J.J. had started to feel restless. Rather than ruining Janey's tour, he'd gone outside to stroll around Franklin Square while she visited and got her fill of the history offered inside the church. City Market was across the way, and he had seen several of the people from the conference going in and out of the stores there.

It had been after four when they returned to their

room. When the phone rang, J.J. pounced on it. "Hello?" he said.

Janey looked inquiringly across the room at him. He mouthed "Korine" and went back to listening.

"Chaz took it pretty well," Korine said. "I think we're going to be okay." She didn't specify how many people "we" included.

"Good," J.J. replied. "Have you seen or heard anything more from Sudley today?"

"He stopped by this afternoon. Had all sorts of questions for Leo. Then he wanted to know who had access to my purse to put that seed packet inside. He's still not sure I didn't do it."

"Yes, he is. Don't worry about that."

"Do you mind if I ask you a question?"

"Fire away," J.J. said.

"If Leo is Holly's father, then that strengthens his motive for killing Dodie, doesn't it?"

Very good question, J.J. thought. *Korine hasn't lost her head.* Out loud, he answered, "Yes, it does. Why do you ask?"

"I'm still not sure how I feel about Leo. Oh, hell. Is Janey there? I tried to get Amilou on the phone and she's out. I need to talk with a woman about this."

"She's right here." J.J. held the phone out for his wife.

Janey hung up after a few minutes and announced, "I'm going up to see her."

"Good," J.J. said. He carefully didn't ask her what Korine had said. When Janey didn't leave right away, J.J. asked, "Do you want me to go with you?"

"No," she answered, "I don't think she wants you there." She reached over and swung her purse up onto her shoulder and hugged him.

"As long as you'll be with Korine, I think I'm going to head back over to the hospital and try to get in to talk with Sharon. I'll give her your best wishes." Even though he'd been warned away, he still had questions for the Winslows which hadn't been answered.

ONCE AGAIN, Holly was the first member of the family J.J. saw. She was parked in a plastic-covered chair in the hallway outside the Coronary Care Unit. She'd pulled her legs up so that she could hug them to her thin frame. Her baggy sweatshirt swallowed her. Holly was concentrating so hard on what was going on inside the unit that she barely registered his presence.

J.J. put his hand on her shoulder. "What is it?" he asked.

Holly began to rock herself. "I think my mom is going to die."

J.J. had to lean down to hear her next words.

"Whoever killed cousin Dodie is killing my mom, too."

Her use of the present tense was unsettling. J.J. gave the door an involuntary glance, as if the murderer would come out at any minute to announce he'd finished his work.

When the door actually opened, J.J. jumped back, his hand dropping away from Holly. A nurse scurried out, carrying several tubes of blood. She cast a sympathetic glance in Holly's direction but didn't stop.

"What happened?" he asked.

"Her heart stopped beating."

"How long ago?" J.J. glanced down at his watch.

"I don't know. Forever! They won't tell me how she's doing. They won't let me see her. Every time I go in, someone pushes me back out."

"It's a good sign that they're still working with her," J.J. lied.

The expression in Holly's pale blue eyes, rimmed with smudged mascara, told him that she knew he was lying. J.J.'s eyes slid away from that scornful contact. A little ways down the hall was an open door to the waiting room. He went and hefted one of the chairs, returned, and sat down next to the girl. She deserved better than to wait this out alone.

A little while later a man wearing a white lab coat came out. He stood uncertainly on the threshold of the unit and looked at Holly. "Is your father here?" he asked.

"No, but I know where to find him," she answered. Unfolding her legs, she stood up unsteadily.

"Your mom's stabilized, for now. If you give us a few minutes we'll be ready for you to come in and see her."

Holly stood still, arms hugging herself for dear life. She turned a stunned visage to J.J.

"Are you going to call your dad?"

"No." Holly did one of her personality flops, going from grieving to rebellious in five seconds flat. "He couldn't bother to stick around. I see no reason to let him know what's going on."

"You didn't tell him that your mother's heart stopped?"

Holly gave him an unreadable look. "He wasn't here. I doubt he cares."

"I've met him. He cares."

The nurse came out and escorted Holly in to see her mother. She left without a backwards glance. J.J. waited a while, but when Holly didn't come back out, he decided to return to the hotel. Sharon certainly wasn't going to be up to talking, and he wanted to think on Holly's odd behavior before tackling her again.

He ran into Sudley in the parking lot. "Sharon just coded," J.J. informed him.

"She didn't die, did she?"

"No. Holly's in with her now."

"And Winslow?"

"Not here. Holly didn't notify him about Sharon's condition. That young lady's what I'd call unstable."

"How's that?"

"She was genuinely upset about her mom. And she sat there, chewing her nails—alone—while her dad's somewhere else. Holly said she knew where he was, but she didn't even try to reach him. You don't suppose she thinks he tried to kill her mother?"

"You know, that's occurred to me." Sudley squinted up at the building. He tugged the cap back down over his eyes to shield them from the glare of the late-afternoon sun. "I got Holly's birth certificate."

"And," J.J. prompted impatiently.

"And her proud papa is George Winslow."

"Damn, another great idea shot to dust. I thought for sure that Holly was Dodie and Leo's child."

Sudley smiled. "Just be sure and let me know if any other ideas pop into your head. You're pretty good."

"Thanks," J.J. said, surprised by the frank look that Sudley had leveled at him. "Will do. And, Sudley?"

"Yes." The detective sounded resigned.

"I know what a pain it is, having to tiptoe around telling me to go to hell. I appreciate it that you haven't done so yet."

"My pleasure," Sudley said. He raised a hand in farewell and walked up the sidewalk toward the front door of the hospital.

J.J. got into his car and started back to the hotel. He was due to go on duty again on Wednesday. He and Janey would have to leave Savannah the next day in order to have enough time to drive back and be ready to take his shifts. There was no way he could leave the department under the care and feeding of his second any longer than that. He hoped Sudley wrapped it up before the day was out.

While stopped at the first traffic light, he wondered if they'd ever know for certain who had done this. His money was still on Sharon or Leo, but with Holly's abrupt mood swings, she was, probably, equally as liable to have murdered Dodie as her mother was. Could her raw emotion over her mother's illness be the result of fear, or guilt? J.J. narrowed his eyes and stared out the side window. A car horn behind him recalled him to the road. He stepped on the gas and moved on.

He stopped at a gas station on the way back to fill the tank. While there, he pulled out his wallet and took out the slip of paper with Chaz's new phone number on it. Crossing the oil-stained concrete, J.J. picked up the pay phone. The metal cord came away with the receiver. J.J. stared at it for a minute, then went inside. The door shut behind him, ringing the bell hanging on the top of it.

The clerk came out from behind a towering stack of soda cases. "Yeah?" he said languidly.

"Can I borrow your phone? The one outside is broken."

"Don't I know it," the man replied. He went behind the counter and got out an old-fashioned black rotary phone. "Hey, don't knock it," the man told J.J. when he saw the look on his face. "Works better than that expensive job they put in out there."

"I believe you." J.J. picked up and dialed. The slow series of clicks brought back memories of home. Party lines and dialing Rhonda for that first date back in junior high. He shook off the nostalgia when Richard picked up on his end. "Janey and I have to head back in the morning. I thought I'd get in touch with you and make sure you think that Korine is in the clear."

"You know she is," Richard replied. "Sudley called me this morning to ask if he could talk to her. I went over, and he was very conciliatory." He covered the mouthpiece and spoke to someone on the other end of the line. "Chaz wants a word."

After a pause, Chaz said, "You're leaving?"

"Is there any way I could come over there? There's something I'd like to get straight with you before I leave town."

"Sure," Chaz said, then gave him directions.

J.J. hung up the phone to find the clerk watching him warily. Rapidly, he reviewed his conversation to see what would cause this about-face in the man's attitude. The words *in the clear* echoed in J.J.'s head. He resisted smiling at the man as he left thirty-five cents on the counter for him. Let him wonder.

He followed the directions that Chaz had given him and arrived at the house a few minutes later. J.J. saw a note on the front door that looked like a citation. If it was for the trim, the house deserved it. Chaz had told him to go around back. The boy was braver than he looked. The stairs swayed slightly under J.J. As he knocked on the door, he wondered if there was another exit.

Richard opened the door on J.J.'s second knock. The apartment was neater than J.J.'s place had ever been during his stint as a bachelor. He sat gingerly on the sofa, hoping that the vibrant colors wouldn't rub off on his faded jeans.

"What's on your mind?" Richard said.

"First of all, I suppose I should congratulate you both."

"I'm glad Korine told you," Richard said formally. He reached out and took Chaz's hand. "Is that what you came to talk with us about?"

"No. Actually, I've got some reservations about leaving before this case is done." J.J. avoided looking at the two joined hands.

Chaz smiled wryly and let go of Richard. J.J. relaxed. He knew better, but some things just can't be helped. He sat back and pulled one booted foot up on his knee. Chaz's grin widened.

J.J.'s next words wiped the smile off his face. "When Sudley talked to your mom, did he say anything about letting her go home?"

"No," Chaz answered slowly. "Did he say anything to you?" he asked Richard.

"No," Richard said.

"Think he's still holding her in reserve?" Chaz asked.

"No." Richard was firm in his answer.

J.J. was beginning to think that Richard was always firm, even when he didn't know the answer. J.J. said, "You're going to have to dig and find out which of these people killed Dodie."

"I know you've had trouble letting him do it, but that's Sudley's job," Richard said.

J.J. looked him in the eye. "Yes, it is. But how do you expect it will affect your law practice knowing that your lover's mother is still considered a possible murderess?"

"As I said, Korine isn't considered to be a suspect any longer." Richard was definite in his answer. "I spoke with Sudley late this afternoon to let him know what Korine had shared with us." Richard broke off to exchange a sympathetic look with Chaz. "Fortunately she'd already told him the whole story."

"That business with Leo in high school?"

"Korine let Leo take the blame for her part in the wreck, and it's been gnawing at her all this time."

"I know," J.J. said. "I was there when she told Sudley. No wonder she's so good at keeping secrets. She's held her own for all that time."

"Secrets can be like millstones," Richard said, glancing over at Chaz as he spoke. "I wouldn't be surprised if she doesn't cut loose a bit, now that she's handed it off to others."

"Leo was the only one who was punished back then, wasn't he?" J.J. hadn't thought to ask Korine and Leo that question earlier.

"Yes," Chaz said. "They'd agreed to let people think that Leo was driving. But Grandmom could tell they were lying, so Aunt Kindra told Grandmom the truth. The fact that Leo left town the next day was confirmation in lots of people's minds that he was guilty."

"Later, when Leo was arrested for something else," Richard explained, "that earlier wreck was an unofficial factor in his being sent to reform school instead of being let off with a warning. Korine didn't even know about it. One more thing that her mother decided she couldn't handle. When Korine didn't respond to Leo's letters, it must have made the hell he was going through even worse."

Richard's dark eyes had softened as he watched Chaz. Even while monitoring Chaz's state of mind, he'd summed things up pretty well. J.J. could see why Sudley respected him. Richard was pretty discerning. He must be a hell of a person to face in court.

Chaz spoke up, obviously defensive on his mother's behalf. "She didn't want to tell you because she was afraid of losing your friendship. Obstruction of justice, even that long ago, is something she figured you'd frown upon."

"I guess it doesn't matter that much, but I would

have liked to have known earlier," J.J. said as gracefully as he could. It did matter. But not nearly as much as it would have if she'd done it on his watch. He knew Korine. He knew her to be incapable of shifting blame for anything to someone else. Having done it once, she'd evidently learned something invaluable from the burden she'd carried with the memory of that deed. It was entirely possible that her knack for gentle listening, and the way she cut through to the heart of problems, was a result of that experience.

"What did Sudley say about this?"

"Pretty much what you said. He also said that he'd be very glad to see this case resolved. He's more than a little sweet on Korine." Richard smiled.

Chaz's face was a picture. "No way!" he exclaimed.

"Tricky for him—to find he likes one of the suspects. He's got good taste. I figured as much," J.J. said, as if he'd known all along.

"Liar," Chaz said, laughing.

J.J. smiled. "Yeah, I know. But the thought was pure."

Even Richard laughed at that one.

"So what does Sudley have?" J.J. asked. "He's been very courteous lately, but not terribly forthcoming with any information."

"You know as well as I do that he wouldn't rule Mother out without a very good idea who did it. You just don't want to leave, in the middle of an investigation."

J.J. grinned sheepishly at the direct hit. "I don't think Sudley's foolish. I think he knows who did it, and I want to know what he knows."

"So you'll know who he knows did it?" Richard asked mockingly.

"Don't be fresh with me," J.J. said. "You've worked with enough policemen to know that any case eventually becomes personal enough that you have to solve it, even if you can't prove it in a court of law."

Richard got up, went into the other room, and came back with a box of papers. "I brought these home to look at one last time before we went back into the office tomorrow. Here's what we have." He pulled out a sheaf of fax sheets.

Many of them were things that J.J. had seen before, thanks to his snooping through Sudley's papers after the detective's interview with Janey. He took his time going through them, though, because he might have missed something.

"Here." Chaz had sorted through one stack and handed J.J. a sheet of paper. On it were notes of the locations of the suspects throughout the day on Saturday.

J.J. looked at Chaz. "Yours, or Sudley's?"

"Mine. It got mixed in these when we boxed them up this morning."

According to the sheet, both Korine and Sharon were pretty much accounted for all day by other people. Both Leo and Holly had gaps in their stories. In addition, there was a large chunk of time in which they both said they'd stood in the lobby talking, but none of the other witnesses' reports mentioned them as being there at the time they had said they were.

"This is good," J.J. said. "So, what were they talking

about? Or were they really talking? Think one of them is covering for the other one?"

"The question is," Chaz said, "which one is covering and which one is guilty?"

"You know," J.J. said, "Sudley told me a little while ago that Holly was the Winslows' daughter."

"What?" Chaz exclaimed, looking up from his share of papers. "I wonder why he told you that. Holly is George Winslow's daughter, but Dodie is her birth mother. I was there collecting some other things on another case when Winslow came in this afternoon. Evidently, Sudley had called him and asked him some questions about Holly's birth certificate. Winslow told Sudley that Holly found out a few weeks ago. She needed another copy of her birth certificate for the school. The Winslows had doctored the one they'd originally showed her. Holly had submitted the doctored one to Davidson on admission. Of course, she didn't know that at the time. For some reason, the school had misplaced it. They called her and asked her to submit another one. Instead of calling her parents, she sent off for an original and discovered the truth."

Richard found what he was looking for and handed it to J.J. It was a record of admission to Memorial Health University Hospital for an overdose of sleeping pills. Dated two weeks prior to the conference. For Holly Winslow.

NINETEEN

KORINE SHIVERED in the chill as she turned up the temperature setting on the air conditioner. Outside her window, Savannah was getting ready to go home from work. Chaz and Richard had left an hour earlier, promising to meet her for dinner around seven.

She'd told them. It hadn't been nearly as bad as she'd thought it would be. As Chaz pointed out, the wreck was long ago, and she'd paid the price of the guilt for a long while afterward. Even more remarkable than Chaz's calm acceptance of her story was that Leo held no grudge about having taken the blame for Nate's death.

Korine got up and walked over to the phone on the bar. She needed to talk with someone objective. She picked up the phone to call Janey and J.J. No answer.

That figured. There was a general lack of definitive answers in her life right then. For instance: All the questions that meeting Leo Gilcrest brought up for her. The relationship between Richard and Chaz. Janey's quest for motherhood that they'd spent so much time discussing earlier when they'd finished discussing the first two questions. It was like someone had handed her a Magic 8-Ball, stuck on ANSWER INCONCLUSIVE, DO OVER.

Some things couldn't be fixed by doing them over. Nate was still dead. They had all been drinking, and if any one of the four of them was going to drive, it had to be Korine. A better choice would have been to call someone else. It was still her fault. Leo's forgiveness had not absolved her.

Korine lifted her head and stared out over the trees, as she had so often in the last three days. Even if he hadn't given her absolution, Leo might be able to give her something else. She'd been grieving for Charlie for seven years. As Janey had pointed out, she was a widow. But she hadn't died herself. Perhaps, despite their past, something good could be forged between a grown Korine and Leo.

She swung around and strode across the room. She'd spent entirely too much time lately thinking and not near enough time enjoying the people that she loved. Or even allowing herself the opportunity to discover people that she might love.

Korine flung open the closet. The restaurant Leo had chosen for that night was supposed to be the best in Savannah. When she packed, she had stuck in something for emergency purposes. She'd never in her wildest dreams imagined that the clothing emergency would be to go on a double date with her son. At least she'd brought the dress for it.

Half an hour later, she pulled the strap up on the high heels she'd also thrown in her suitcase, just in case. She hadn't worn heels for a very long time. Who knew what devil had tempted her to tuck them in at the last minute. Checking herself in the mirror, she decided she would do. She picked up the new purse that Chaz had bought her that afternoon. It didn't match the dress, but at least it wasn't broken. She let herself out and took the elevator down to meet Leo.

He was waiting for her by the post in front of the elevator. His eyebrows went up in a very satisfactory way when he saw her. "The girl I remember couldn't have pulled that dress off," he said in her ear as he kissed her cheek in greeting.

Several people in the lobby stared. Javier, behind his counter, gave her a thumbs-up sign before going back to work. Korine held her head high. Who cared what people thought?

As Leo held the door open for her to go out to the car, Korine still felt her cheeks burning. A small voice inside her was calling her "hussy." She shushed it. Janey was right. It had been a long time since Charlie died. The part of Korine that died with him had been mourned properly. It was time to start healing. They got into Leo's car.

"Is it far?"

"Not too far. Savannah's just the right size. Big enough for variety, small enough so that driving time isn't ever too long."

"What kind of landscaping do you do?" Korine asked, trying for an innocent subject.

"Businesses mostly. It's challenging to try and put something in that's original but doesn't die when it's put in next to a sidewalk. Then there's the issue of what color goes best with their logo."

Korine laughed. "We do houses. Although, we did redo the county courthouse gardens last fall. I never knew how strongly people could feel about the color of pansies."

Leo's teeth flashed as he negotiated a turn. "Do you like dogs?" he asked suddenly.

"Yes, but I have a cat," Korine replied cautiously.

He took one hand off the wheel and passed it over his head, smoothing an imaginary strand of hair into place. "I feel like I'm back in high school and going out for the first time ever," Leo said. "I don't know what to talk about."

"I know." Korine sat for a moment, watching the houses stream by as she thought. "Tell me about your wife," she said, turned to watch Leo's profile in the gathering darkness.

"Fiona?" Leo said, startled. He turned to meet her look, then swore as he stomped on the brakes to avoid hitting a black Volvo stopped at the red light in front of them. "Sorry," he said.

"I'm sorry," Korine said. "I didn't mean to distract you."

"You can't help that," he replied, letting the car inch forward through the intersection as the light changed. Korine could feel a telltale blush creeping up her neck. It vanished with his next words. "Fiona was fair, tall, and slim. She had an absolute genius with flowers. Anything would grow for her."

Korine self-consciously took stock of her graying dark hair, her medium height, her inner thighs, and the number of plants that had died in their pots, over the years, before they ever got planted in the ground. Not a good idea on a first date. "Go on," she said, very sorry she had asked.

"I still remember how I felt the first time you smiled at me. Mr. Matthews's fifth-period science class." Leo looked over at her and smiled. "And that dress isn't bad either."

Korine smiled back. She put a hand out to steady herself as they hit a bump.

"Sorry about that," he said. "But, at least we're here."

The valet parking attendant let her out, and she stood studying Leo as he exchanged keys and ticket with the young man. He was still very handsome. Still very charming. But there was something harder about him too. Korine was willing to bet that life hadn't been all sweetness and light for him the last four decades. The correctional institution would be difficult to gloss over when applying for jobs.

She took the arm he offered her, and they entered the building. The lighting was so low as to almost be considered dim. She could hear the patrons' swirl of conversation through the open door to the dining room, but it was hushed, hardly louder than the soft jazz Korine heard coming from the speaker above her head.

Richard and Chaz were in the bar when Korine and Leo got there. Leo took her elbow to steer her through the door to greet them. Korine pulled her elbow gently out of his grasp and steered herself.

He chuckled behind her. "Still independent, as always."

She smiled over her shoulder at him.

Richard plainly approved of her attire; Chaz, just as plainly, did not. Neither of them was thrilled with Leo. By the time they sat down to dinner, Korine realized what an error in judgment she had made in trying to resurrect her relationship with Leo at the same time that she tried to forge one with Richard.

By the time they all stood to leave, Korine's head ached from all the unspoken currents surrounding their table. Richard leaned over and touched Chaz on the sleeve, then leaned in to whisper something unobtrusively in his ear. Standing next to Leo, Korine could feel his arm stiffen.

It dawned on her that Leo didn't know how to behave around the other two men. Every time they turned to each other, he had tensed, as if they'd display their affection in public and embarrass him. Korine felt superior for a moment—until she realized that she, too, had tensed the same way that Leo did. At that moment, too, she realized that the four of them hadn't exchanged any conversation since they'd left the table. Waiting for the cars, the silence was deafening.

Korine broke the silence. "Chaz, would you mind if I stopped by your office in the morning? I'd really like to see it."

"Sure," Chaz said. His smile softened the tense lines on his face.

Korine made a second effort and turned to Richard. "I'd like to stop by and see your office too," she said.

Richard smiled slightly, acknowledging her effort.

"I'd love to show you around. Much better that you should do so as my guest than as a potential inmate."

Leo put his arm around her as she gasped.

"Richard!" Chaz said.

"I didn't mean it that way." For the first time since she had met him, Korine saw Richard dumfounded.

She shrugged off her hurt feelings and put a hand out to touch Richard's arm. "It's all right. We're all a little edgy tonight," she said.

"You've got that right," Leo whispered as he handed the valet the ticket for his car.

A second valet, grinning from ear to ear, climbed out of a silver Miata he'd pulled in behind Leo's Cadillac. Richard went around and stood next to the open door of the sports coupe. "Tomorrow," he said. "Come around lunch and I'll give you the guided tour."

Korine and Chaz hugged. "I'll call you in the morning," she said.

"He's not all bad," Chaz said in her ear. He released her and slid into the passenger seat.

As the men drove away, Leo expelled a long sigh. "I hope I didn't blow that."

"It was difficult, wasn't it?" Korine equivocated.

"Okay, I blew it, but you'll forgive me by going to have a cup of coffee?"

"Sure," Korine said as they got into the car and pulled away.

"Back to the hotel?" Leo asked.

"Actually," Korine said after taking a deep breath, "I'd like to see your place, if you don't mind."

Leo didn't answer, just flipped on his turn signal and pressed the gas.

Five minutes later, he pulled up in front of a two-story brick town house in the city's historic district. Tastefully expensive, there wasn't any magenta paint in sight.

Coming around the car to help Korine out, Leo laughed when he found that she was already out and shutting the door. "I keep forgetting how different you are from the way you used to be," he said.

As he fitted the key in the front door, Korine said, "It's been a long time. I've had to learn to do a good many things for myself other than open doors and scoot my own chair in at the table."

Leo gave her a steady look as he held the door open for her. "I'm old-fashioned that way. I hope you don't mind," he said.

"I'm sorry. Nerves talking, not me." Now that she was inside, Korine was nervous. Much more so than she had expected to be. The entryway was done in a lavender rose wallpaper. She hated it.

"Fiona had strong color sense. She never would have let somebody put this stuff in. I hired a decorator. She had strange ideas, but without Fiona I really didn't care as much." He put his keys in a small silver ashtray on the hall table. "The kitchen's through here. Is it all right with you if we sit in there for coffee?"

It was perfect. After the hallway and the glimpse of the living room done in pink orchids, Korine was relieved to find the kitchen plain white and blue. Not a flower in sight. She must have sighed.

"I know." Leo stood looking beyond her to the dining room, in which Korine could see a row of yellow day lilies blooming along the wallpaper border above the chair rail. "I do a lot of my consulting with clients here at home. The decorator felt it helped my business to do the decorating with a floral theme." He pulled out the top of the Mr. Coffee and dumped an old filter in the trash. Filling the pot with water, he poured it in and flipped the switch. He indicated the caned chairs on either side of the maple drop-leaf table. They sat.

"You must have loved her very much."

"Yes," Leo replied. "I did. She helped me make something of myself. I tended to think of myself as a convict, which I was in a sense—but not really."

"I'm glad you had someone," she said.

"It could have been you."

His words caught Korine like a slap. She felt her cheeks burn as if he'd actually made contact. Forcing herself to remain still, she looked back at him. "I told you already how sorry I am."

"I wasn't passing blame," he said.

"Good," Korine said sharply.

"Coffee's on," Leo said and left the table. He poured out two cups and brought them back. He shoved a battered stainless steel sugar bowl over to her. "Do you need milk too?" he asked, as if the previous conversation hadn't occurred.

"No, thank you."

"Did your husband suffer much before he died?"

Korine stirred her coffee. "It wasn't fun," she said.

Lifting the cup, she took a sip. She made a face at the doctored taste.

"You don't like hazelnut?" Leo asked. "I've got regular, but it's instant."

"No, it's fine," she lied. That earlier feeling of cresting a wave and seeing something new and exciting on the far horizon had winked out with Leo's mention of Nate and her failure to support Leo afterward. Making conversation now was like rowing through mud. "I'd better go." She stood, shivering.

Leo looked up at her in surprise. "I'll take you home, of course, if you really want me to. I'd like you to stay."

To Korine's surprise, she sat back down again and picked up her cup. The second sip was better than the first. "Sharon lives just down the street, doesn't she?" Korine asked.

"Yes. I hadn't realized that, of course, when I bought the house. You can imagine how I felt when Dodie walked up to me two weeks after I'd moved in. I thought I'd been able to put her behind me."

"I thought I saw something in her. Some yearning for friendship."

"It was an illusion. Dodie could turn the vulnerability on and off."

Korine opened her mouth to tell Leo about her dream. At the last minute, she decided that she didn't want to talk anymore about Dodie, and she shut her mouth. She covered for the gaff by shivering. "Do you have a sweater I could borrow? I'm not used to going in and out of the air-conditioning. I think I might be coming down with something."

She followed him out to the hallway but stopped short of trailing up the stairs after him. Instead, she went into the living room while he went on up the steps. Turning on a light, she walked around and looked at the family photos. A younger Leo grinned, holding up what was surely a prizewinning fish. In the next frame, Leo, in a white tuxedo with tails, looked self-consciously into the camera. Next to him stood a stunning willowy blonde. Fiona was beautiful. And they looked radiant together. No wonder he missed her so much.

A stereo sat on a lower shelf of the bookcase next to the fireplace. Korine touched the POWER button. Music might make conversation easier. There was a tape in the player, so she pushed the PLAY button.

"You don't understand!" Dodie's angry voice filled the room.

She pressed STOP, hoping that Leo hadn't heard. Heavy footfalls sounded on the stairs behind Korine. She slipped the tape out of the player, turned the stereo off, and ran through the dining room back into the kitchen. She looked up from her purse when he entered the room.

"Thank you," she said, still shaking as he tucked the sweater in around her shoulders.

"Can I help you find something?" Leo asked, when Korine stuck her hand farther down inside her purse.

"No, I've got it." She pulled out a bottle of aspirin she kept in the side pocket. "I really do think I'm coming down with something."

"Maybe I'd better take you back to the hotel." Leo looked genuinely concerned.

Korine stood abruptly, her knee bumping the table, knocking over the cup of coffee. It ran off the edge of the table onto the front of her dress. "Don't worry," she said. "I'll put it out for the hotel to clean for me tonight. They'll take care of it."

"I've got tonic," Leo said playfully.

Korine managed a laugh. "I don't think this dress will take anything else liquid. Dry Clean Only."

"Got everything?" Leo asked as he put his hand under her elbow to steer her out the door.

"Got everything," Korine repeated. What she didn't say, what she didn't know, was what to do with "everything" once she got back to the hotel.

TWENTY

"WELL, I WAS RIGHT about Holly's stability," J.J. said to himself. He'd left Chaz and Richard getting ready for dinner with Korine and Leo Gilcrest. His nose still wrinkled when he thought about it. The four of them together at a table should be mighty interesting.

J.J. had brought along Holly's admission form when he'd raced back to the hospital hoping to catch Sudley. But the detective, it seemed, had given up on the Winslows and had retreated to his paperwork in his office. So J.J. sat in the ICU waiting room, tastefully decorated walls closing in around him, trying to decide if he should try to reach Sudley by phone, or if he should go ahead and wait for morning.

He'd tried to see Sharon earlier, only to be shown the door by the nursing staff, who were all involved in some emergency. The family, he was told as the door shut in his face, had been asked to leave earlier. Evidently Holly and her father still weren't getting along.

Janey poked her head in the door. J.J.'s eyes narrowed as he regarded her.

"What?" she said rebelliously.

"I thought I told you to stay away from this family."

"You're not my daddy," she retorted, color suffusing her face.

J.J. took that in, then sat back in his chair, transferring his attention to the piece of paper in his hand. As long as she was there, he might as well share it with her. Leaning forward again, he thrust the piece of paper out at Janey. "What do you make of this?"

Janey scanned it. "Where is Holly right now?"

"Probably down in the cafeteria with her father. The staff kicked the two of them out a while ago for upsetting Sharon. They've been at odds all day." Shortly, J.J. outlined how he'd found Holly alone while Sharon was so ill, and how he'd stayed with her.

Janey's warm look approved his actions.

"Holly said something very interesting. She told me that the person who killed Dodie was killing her mother."

"You think she was talking about herself? A bid to be stopped?" Janey's tone was unbelieving. "She could just have easily been talking about Sharon herself."

J.J. said, "It will be very interesting to see who winds up in jail for this murder."

"Why are you so sure that she's not the killer?"

"I'm not." For the first time, J.J. heard doubt behind her words. "I just hate for a young girl to have done this. Such a young life to be wasted."

J.J. hauled himself up out of the chair and reached for the pay phone on the wall. Dialing Sudley's office, he asked for the detective. The two of them waited while Sudley was fetched.

"Sudley? J.J. Bascom. Why didn't you tell me that Holly Winslow had tried to commit suicide recently?" When the detective didn't answer, J.J. continued, "Richard gave me a copy of her birth certificate. You deliberately misled me, didn't you?"

"I didn't try to mislead you. I just didn't tell you everything. What I have been trying to do is to get you to leave me alone so that I can get on with it. So far I haven't been very successful. You're damned stubborn." Sudley's voice had risen.

Gingerly feeling his way through this man's emotional land mines, J.J. said, "I'm not meddling. You asked me to let you know if there was anything I found that you might need."

"I know you're not meddling, but I'm spending as much time talking to you as I am investigating." Sudley cleared his throat. "But as long as you've got me on the phone, you might as well tell me what you've found," he commanded.

"Correct me if I'm wrong, but Holly just found out that her mom isn't her mom, and that her dad slept with her cousin who is really her mother. Right?"

"Right," Sudley replied cautiously.

"Then she tried to kill herself. Which I find perfectly understandable. Just saying that whole relationship thing out loud makes me crazy. The thing is: What did she use?" J.J. asked.

"How the hell should I know? Does it matter?" The sound of rustling papers filled J.J.'s ears. "Damn." Sudley paused. "You are good." As a compliment, it fell rather flat. Sudley didn't sound very thrilled to admit it. "She ate a couple of leaves off the oleander shrub in her backyard."

J.J.'s lacerated feelings blew. He felt his face heat up. Janey reached a hand out to try and stem his temper. It didn't work. "So you had all this in the file and haven't hauled her in for questioning?"

Sudley met J.J.'s anger with irritation of his own. "First of all, she has been questioned—several times. Why do you suppose her father hates the hell out of me? So far as I know, she's cooperating. I can't 'haul her in' until I get some evidence to charge her with something. I don't happen to have any. Evidence, in case you've forgotten, is what I have to have to make an arrest. Just because she ate the same thing that poisoned her cousin and probably her mother doesn't make her guilty. The whole lot of them knew what she'd done—and how it affected her. All of them," Sudley emphasized.

J.J., yielding to the steady pressure that Janey's nails were making in his arm, took a few deep breaths before replying. "Frustrating," he said through clenched teeth.

The blue streak that Sudley sent over the wires should have gotten him a citation from the FCC.

J.J. didn't stop pushing, even then. "You've said yourself repeatedly that I have good insights. Don't keep me in the dark; use me. I'm not doing this to show you up; I'm doing this because I care that whoever did this gets caught and punished. Just like you do."

Sudley didn't reply, and J.J. heard the man's breathing come heavily over the wire. When he finally did re-

spond, his tone had altered subtly. There was resigna-
tion there, if it still lacked respect. "I guess this means
I'd better get back over there and talk to Miss Winslow
again in the morning."

J.J. stifled a sound of impatience.

Sudley responded to it anyway. "I haven't slept in
two days. If I don't sleep, then I won't be near as tactful as it's going to take to get the Winslows to cooper-
ate. Personally," he added, "I still think Gilcrest did it
so that he could have a clear path to your friend. But I'll
follow up with Holly tomorrow."

"Do that," J.J. told Sudley.

J.J. turned to Janey and handed her the car keys.
She'd taken a cab over, and he wanted her gone in case
things got messy. It took a good solid ten minutes of per-
suading, and by the end, it was the wrong person who
was persuaded. Janey took the keys, but she stayed.

As he sat there, restlessly crossing and uncrossing his
leg over his knee, J.J. thought more about things. Something was bugging him, but he still couldn't put his finger on what it was about Leo that bugged him so much.
He hated it when a case got to the point where he thought
he knew who had done it but his intuition sent up red flags.

"Talk to me," Janey said.

"I'm sure Holly killed Dodie. I just can't get around
the fact that Gilcrest says that he was with her at the time
that Dodie was arguing with the person we assume was
the murderer. That, and I think that Javier saw them both
at the time the murder occurred. Then there's the fact
that Dodie sent the same poison to Sharon."

"The only male unaccounted for is Sharon's husband," Janey pointed out. "He and Dodie could have been working together, then had a falling out, and he killed Dodie after she'd arranged for Sharon to receive the candy. Or he could have done it to protect Holly."

J.J. narrowed his eyes as he thought about that. "I really wish that technician had shown up. Then we'd have a tape to compare to the various people involved and we could figure this out easily."

Janey just looked at him.

He snorted at his own statement. "I know. It's never easy."

She stood up. "I'm going to see if they're letting people in to see Sharon yet."

J.J. stood up, too, and followed his wife out into the corridor. The floor was eerily quiet. They turned in the door of Sharon's unit and stopped a nurse.

"You're back?" She acknowledged J.J.'s presence. "She's fine now, poor thing."

"What was going on? Has anything else happened?"

"Just now? No, that was somebody else. Mrs. Winslow's fine. Only thing wrong with her is that her family's a mess right now." The young woman threw a pitying glance toward the curtain drawn in front of Sharon's bed. "They couldn't wait until they got home to argue; the pair of them had to do it in front of a woman who nearly died this afternoon." Even though the nurse couldn't have been more than in her mid-twenties, her tone said that she'd seen it all.

J.J. stopped the nurse as she turned away. "What were they arguing about?"

"The daughter was accusing her daddy of trying to kill her mom."

Janey and J.J. looked at each other, then back at the nurse. "Are you sure?" J.J. asked.

"Oh yeah, real sure," she replied.

An alarm sounded and she looked across the desk to another, older, woman in scrubs standing there, finger on the monitor alarm button. "Just Mr. Greville's pacemaker. Don't you worry."

The young nurse delivered a final observation before going in to check on her patient. "That girl all but accused her father of tryin' to kill her mother. We finally got the supervisor to come make them leave because Mrs. Winslow was having arrhythmias just listening to them."

J.J. and Janey walked over and pulled the curtain aside to reveal a sleeping Sharon. Her face looked naked with her oversized bifocals. A jaunty green line bounced its way across a screen above her head. As the nurse had said, neither Holly nor Winslow was with Sharon.

J.J. stood next to the bed. He reached out, then drew his hand back. Janey shook her head. J.J. didn't need her to warn him off. If Sharon had arrhythmias with Holly and Winslow arguing, then he had no business trying to get her to answer any questions right now. Frowning, he stopped short of touching Sharon, and he turned to go.

"Let's try the cafeteria," Janey suggested in a low voice. "We won't have to bother Sharon at all that way."

Sharon's eyes opened. She reached for the call button when she saw the two of them looming over her.

"I'm sorry, Sharon." Janey stepped up to the bedside. "We wanted to come say hello and wish you a speedy recovery. But you've had a pretty rough day. We'll leave you alone."

It was the right thing to have said. Sharon relaxed and touched the button that brought her head up instead of calling the nurse. "Thank you for coming," she said.

It's an odd thing with some women, J.J. thought. *The dance of social mores is stronger than their wish to tell someone to go to hell.* He said, "I'll go down and get Holly and your husband to come back up."

Sharon stiffened. "Don't bother with them, they'll be back soon enough." The line bouncing along above her head wavered as she spoke, as if reflecting her uncertainty.

J.J. said, "You aren't afraid of them are you?"

"Holly loves me. She's my daughter in heart, soul, and mind. She would never, never hurt me." The intensity in Sharon's eyes faded as the line above her head became erratic. A beeping sounded out at the desk.

Janey grabbed J.J.'s arm and hauled him out of the room.

The young woman who had spoken with them earlier thrust past them, dragging a big red tool cart with her. She spat out, "Great, just what we need is for her to code again after all she's been through. Can't you people give it a rest!"

A steady stream of people came through the doorway

from the hall. Sharon's bed was soon surrounded by busy hospital staff.

"What do you think you're doing?" Janey hissed.

If J.J. had wondered what would happen when Janey found the strength that anger could bring, he knew it now. Holding onto his wrist with a grip that he never would have credited to her, she held him back from the elevator and said, "You think that asking questions, of a woman so ill that the staff chased her own family out, is acceptable? Even Detective Sudley knew enough to leave it for tonight. People are part of the human race, not just a bunch of suspects lined up across a platform waiting to be identified for their crimes."

He looked down at Janey, whose face was suffused with righteous anger. Slowly, his own anger at her words faded, replaced by something much more complex and humbling. He had been so focused on the whodunit portion of the recent events, that he hadn't taken the time to step back and see the effects that Dodie's murder had left on all the people involved, including his own wife.

He apologized, then said, "Shouldn't we go tell Winslow and Holly that Sharon may need them?"

Janey turned and walked toward the elevator. Her back was still stiff with anger. J.J. wasn't completely forgiven yet. He trotted along after her.

They found both Holly and her father sitting at a table in the corner of the deserted cafeteria, each nursing a cup of cold coffee. They'd obviously been there a while. Equally obvious, father and daughter had forged a truce, no longer exhibiting the behavior that had gotten them banished from the unit upstairs.

The two heads swung toward them, united in resentment of the interruption.

"Sharon's having difficulty again," Janey said.

Winslow stood abruptly. Holly followed close on his heels as the two of them raced for the stairs. Janey held J.J. back as he tried to follow.

"Leave them be." She stood there, his wife, between him and the chance to talk with Holly about her birth parents and how that affected her.

He thought about that wavering green line above Sharon's head and what Janey had said about his drive for the truth. He nodded his head. "You're right," J.J. said. "Let's go."

Janey pulled out the car keys and led the way to the parking lot.

TWENTY-ONE

KORINE WAS WAITING in the hotel's lobby when J.J. and Janey arrived. She looked like hell. Dinner must have been even worse than J.J. had expected it would be. She shook her head in response to his questions about the meal.

Janey gave him the same impatient look he'd encountered over Sharon's bedside. She might as well have said it out loud: *Too many questions!*

Tucking Korine between them, they ushered her upstairs to her room.

Once there, Korine fiddled with her purse, finally coming up with her key-card. She walked in ahead of them and put her purse down on the bar along with a shopping bag she had been carrying from the hotel gift shop.

"I think Leo killed Dodie," Korine said. She'd turned around, both hands braced behind her on the bull-nosed edge of the bar, as if holding herself up.

Janey made negative soothing sounds.

"I mean it!" Korine said. Tears ran down her face and fell, unnoticed. "I found this in his house—it's a tape of the fight from the room where Dodie was killed.

Leo was the one she argued with that morning." Korine plunged her hand into her purse and came up with a battered cassette tape. "I've been afraid to leave it anywhere."

Looking at it, she gripped it with both hands. Reluctantly, she handed it to J.J. Turning once again to the bar, Korine slid a tape player out of the bag and made go-ahead motions with her hands as if absolving herself of the responsibility for having given the tape to him.

J.J. stepped forward and took the tape Korine held out. He placed it in the open cassette holder and snapped it shut. Pressing PLAY, he waited.

"You don't understand," Dodie's voice, grating, compelling, emerged from the tape.

"You stole my daughter's early years from me, and now you're trying to steal her away entirely!" Plainly, the angry male on the tape was Leo Gilcrest.

"Wanting it so," Dodie's voice said, then paused, "won't change things. She's not your child. I told you she was so that you would come back to me. After how you've treated me this weekend, I don't want you anymore. Holly and I will be just fine on our own."

J.J. stopped the tape. "We're going to have to turn this over to Sudley," he said.

"I know." Korine looked miserable.

"Don't you dare feel guilty. Leo's obviously the one who killed her. You heard it!" Janey said.

"Is that an I-told-you-so?" Korine asked wearily.

"No, it isn't, and you know it." Janey didn't back down. "I'm almost as sorry as you are that he did this."

"You don't understand. I was the one who was responsible for Leo's going into Juvenile Detention all those years ago. What if that is what led him to become the sort of man who would do this?"

"Leo made his own choices back then too," J.J. said. "He may have paid heavily, but you didn't make him— or even ask him to, for that matter—take your place behind the wheel. And if he hadn't made a further mistake, then he wouldn't have had to pay such a heavy price. If I know you, you've paid as high a price as Leo did, even if it was paid out in a different coin."

Korine looked at him. The gratitude he saw in her eyes was fleeting—it was soon replaced by a look of self-loathing. Janey put her arms around the devastated woman, letting Korine's tears fall on her shoulder. J.J. walked past the two women and grabbed the phone.

The officer on duty at the desk answered.

"Call Detective Sudley," J.J. requested.

"He's off duty right now. If you leave a message, I'll see that it gets to him."

"I've got something he'll want to see right away."

"Give me your name and phone number," the bored-sounding voice said.

"This is Police Chief J.J. Bascom. You tell Sudley I have the evidence that he said he needed. If he's interested, he'll call me within the next few minutes. Otherwise, I'm going over his head." It was an empty threat, aimed more at the lazy son of a gun manning the night desk than at Sudley.

J.J. could almost hear the man looking through his

mental directory for J.J.'s name. "Yessir," he said, sounding slightly more interested in doing his job than he had before. "Police chief where, sir?"

J.J. hung up the phone. If the man didn't know, he'd be more likely to follow up.

Janey looked up. She was perched on the edge of Korine's chair. Korine's nails had torn a hole in the arm of the chair. J.J. hoped that the hotel wouldn't charge her for recovering it. "How did your dinner with Richard and Chaz go?" Janey asked.

"Let's put it this way," Korine said. "Chaz won't mind at all that Leo's heading back to jail."

"That good?" Janey said.

"It was awful. I didn't know what to say. Leo sure didn't know what to say. And Chaz looked miserable."

"He feeling caught between you and Richard?"

J.J. listened to the women's conversation. Half his mind was racing trying to figure out how Leo had been able to hide the existence of the tape; the other half was worried as hell about Korine. She didn't look good at all. Then there was the fact that Holly had sworn she was with Leo at the time of the actual murder. If Holly wasn't Leo's daughter, then why was she protecting him?

A knock sounded at the door. As Korine stood and smoothed down her dress, J.J. noticed her staring at a dark stain on the hem of her dress. After staring at it a moment, she shrugged and went to answer the door.

"Where is it?" Leo's angry voice sounded as soon as Korine opened the door.

She backed around the corner, Leo bearing down on her, hands outstretched. J.J. started forward and swung Korine behind him.

Leo stopped.

The four of them stood still, a tragic tableau.

Janey was the first to move. "Sit down," she said. "We've already heard the tape." Janey indicated the tape player sitting on the counter.

J.J. looked at her like she'd lost her mind. Here, a murderer had come in and threatened her friend, and Janey invited him to sit down. Next she'd be offering tea and crumpets.

At a movement, J.J. swung his attention back to Leo.

The man raised his hands, palms out. "Let me explain," Leo begged. His eyes rested on Korine, as if J.J. weren't standing protectively between them. J.J. pulled Korine aside and indicated one of the chairs by the window. Leo walked over to it and sat down heavily. He looked up at Korine and sighed. "I guess it's not meant to be—you and me—is it?"

Korine swayed. Janey came over and stood next to her, encircling her friend's waist with a supportive arm. Korine shook her off and walked over to sit in what had become her spot. Less than an arm's length from Leo, she crossed her arms tightly across her chest.

Together, they waited to hear Leo tell his story.

"Dodie told me that Holly was my daughter. So I had coffee with Holly every now and again, 'bumping into her' when she was home from school. I liked her, but I could tell Holly wasn't very happy. Too much of her mother in her to rest content with the way life was."

The memory of George Winslow tossing a similar comment at Holly in the hospital lobby as if impaling her with the comparison came to J.J.'s mind.

"You've heard the tape. I wanted to get something concrete from Dodie saying that Holly was mine. I didn't get it. Dodie kicked me out, so I had to come back later to get the tape."

J.J. stepped forward. "Wait a minute. When was this tape made?" They'd obviously stopped the tape before it ended.

Leo must have immediately realized his mistake. He stood, lunging for the tape player on the bar. J.J. and Leo grappled as each tried to retain possession of the tape player. Suddenly, something hit Leo from behind. He slumped forward into J.J.'s arms.

Behind Leo's still form stood Janey, Gideon Bible raised over her head, ready to deliver a second blow. Slowly, she lowered the Book. "I hit him," she said, voice quavering. Her eyes lit up. "I hit him!" she said, delight lighting her face.

Korine stepped past her to check Leo where J.J. had let him slide to the floor.

"Yes, you did," J.J. said, hugging his wife. He couldn't be prouder of her if she had flown.

Korine stepped over Leo's prone body to the bar. She turned on the tape player.

"Now get out," Dodie's voice came through the whine of the tape, "or I'll tell Korine why you're here."

A pounding sound was followed by the slam of a door. "And don't come crawling back anytime soon!" Dodie shouted. "What are you staring at?" she demanded.

"Who was that?" Korine's voice emerged from the tape.

"Your friends have an indecent idea of what time to come knocking on doors."

The tape fell silent. Leo stirred on the floor. J.J. stood over him.

"This tape is from Saturday morning, isn't it?" Korine said. "That's why I'm on there."

Leo nodded his head wearily. He sat up.

The tape stayed silent. Janey walked over and pressed STOP and then hit the REWIND button.

J.J. hauled Leo to his feet and escorted him to the chair.

Janey made up an ice bag from the ice bucket and applied it to the spot on Leo's head where she had assaulted him.

Korine retreated to her chair, haunted eyes watching her first love as he began to explain his role in Dodie's murder.

TWENTY-TWO

"YOU WANT TO EXPLAIN that?" J.J. asked.

Leo stopped for a minute to search Korine's face. She didn't want to look him in the eyes, but she couldn't seem to turn her head away.

"I taped Dodie early Saturday morning. I'd stopped by, hoping to get her to admit that Holly was my daughter on tape so that I would have some standing with her."

"She's not your daughter. She's Winslow's," J.J. said.

Leo glanced up at him, a look full of defeat. "I've been told."

Janey stirred, going over to sit on the arm of Korine's chair. Korine thankfully clung to her warm hand.

"So when I knew I had to figure out how to provide an alibi for the time Dodie was killed, I used the tape from the voice-activated tape player. I'd put it inside the box with the gift I'd brought for Korine." At Korine's sound of protest, he said, "Just as well you never got it. It was a little personal. It's just that I overheard you telling a girlfriend one time that you really wanted a pink negligee."

"That was in ninth grade!" Korine's exclamation slipped out.

"As I said, I was in love with you from fifth grade on. Anyway," he continued as Korine looked away, "Dodie opened the box and found the tape player. She confronted me with it later in the empty conference room downstairs. That's when she spilled her drink on the tablecloth."

Leo swallowed. "After Dodie died, I set the tape player next to the microphone in that room and fiddled with the wires so that people would think Dodie died later than she did. That way, Holly and I could be upstairs talking about the conference while Dodie was 'overheard' downstairs."

"And you'd already hidden the body in the linen hamper in the hallway?" J.J. asked.

"Yes," Leo said.

Korine rocketed out of her chair and went over to tower over Leo. "But why?" her question was a cry of pain. "Why on earth did you try to frame me for the murder?"

It was Leo's turn not to look her in the eye. "I didn't want to do that."

"Who helped you?" asked Janey in a low voice. "Who put the oleander in Korine's purse? Who put the negligee on Korine's bed?"

Korine saw a shadow pass over Leo's face, and she knew. Once again she was faced with trying to decide whom to protect. Or if she owed either of them protection. Willing Leo to look at her, she was frustrated when his head stayed bowed.

With difficulty, Korine said, "My guess? Holly is the one who killed Dodie. Leo's helping to protect her."

Leo raised his head and met her gaze squarely. Korine's breath caught. Leo didn't have to admit anything to her. He cared for Holly as if she were his daughter. No accident of blood could take that connection from him. Leo had helped Holly, or vice versa, regardless of the cost. In acknowledging Holly's role in Dodie's death, Korine had abdicated the possibility of a relationship between them.

Leo was still the rakish, handsome man he'd always been. The difference was that Korine now saw that Leo wasn't the type of man that she could respect. His actions placed him far beyond the line that she had drawn in her mind. Because of her role in covering up the truth in Nate's death, and the resulting misery she'd lived with all these years, she could not abide fudging the line.

She'd nearly ruined her own sense of justice with her best friend, Amilou, last summer. She wasn't about to bend her convictions for a man she hardly knew anymore. With surprise, Korine even found that she didn't mind the prospect of losing Leo's admiration so much. There were other men she could—and did—respect. Someday, she might even fall in love with one of them.

Another knock sounded at the door. J.J. let Sudley in and brought him up to speed. The detective stuck the tape in a plastic bag that he brought forth from a pocket and read Leo his rights.

Sudley turned to J.J. and said, "I suppose I owe you an apology."

"No, I'd probably have done the same thing if our situations were reversed."

Korine almost felt like smiling over Janey's exasperation at the exchange. Sudley didn't offer either of the women the same courtesy. And he should have. After all, Janey had knocked Leo down when he was trying to maul her husband, and Korine had found the tape and gotten Leo to admit to how and why he'd used the tape to cover up Dodie's death. Korine immediately felt ashamed. Here she was, thinking of credit, and Leo was being led away to jail mainly thanks to her.

After snapping the cuffs on Leo's wrists, Sudley did give Korine a quick glance of approval. "Mrs. McFaile" was all he said. His tone said much more. Korine's eyebrows rose.

Sudley nodded to Janey and J.J. and took Leo out to the hallway, where another policeman stood to help him escort Leo down to the waiting police car.

Leo looked over his shoulder one last time as Sudley led him out the door. His eyes sought Korine, as if looking for absolution. She couldn't give it to him.

Korine had taken years to forgive herself and Leo for their unintentional roles in Nate's death. She wasn't going to make the mistake of sharing his guilt in this instance. Leo had made a decision. A bad one. And he was going to have to live with the consequences.

"Do you think Sudley will get Leo to implicate Holly?" Korine asked.

"People are funny," J.J. responded. "He might, he might not."

"I think Holly will tell them herself," Janey said unexpectedly. "I know that you didn't think very much of her, but she's got a backbone somewhere under all that angst."

Korine tended to disagree with that assessment, but she held her tongue. No sense in antagonizing Janey over something that didn't matter.

"Both of them will pay a tremendous price, even if they never set foot in jail," Korine said. "And I know."

J.J. nodded his head. Meeting his eyes, Korine saw that he understood what she was saying. She was glad that someone did.

A FEW DAYS LATER, Korine woke to hear the radio news announcing that a second suspect, Holly Winslow, had confessed to the murder of Dodie Halloran. She threw back the sheets on the bed in the guest room of Chaz and Richard's apartment. Pulling on her robe, she hurried to the kitchenette. Richard stood there in his cotton pajama bottoms, rumbling through the refrigerator for the carton of milk, which was on the counter behind him.

"Did you hear?" she asked breathlessly.

Richard straightened. His hair stuck up in spikes around his face. "Hear what?"

"Holly confessed. She was the one who killed Dodie, says she didn't mean to, she was just trying to get Dodie to tell the truth about her father. Seems that Holly's relationship with her father was horrible. She liked the prospect of Leo Gilcrest as Daddy far better," Korine said.

"Did you get that from Sudley last night?" Richard asked.

"Radio," she corrected him.

Chaz came into the kitchen and pulled himself up to sit on the counter. He wore the matching top to the pajama bottoms that Richard had on and a pair of purple boxer shorts. It was a tribute to Korine's newly acquired sangfroid that she was able to keep a straight face when the pair of them realized they'd mixed up their clothes.

"You'll have to call Janey and tell her she was right," Richard said.

Janey and J.J. had gone on back home, leaving Korine in Savannah to stay until Sudley cleared her to return home. He'd taken her out to dinner the night before and hadn't asked her a single question to do with the case. Korine had enjoyed it too.

"Holly didn't happen to mention why she also poisoned her mom?" Chaz asked.

"Evidently that really was Dodie. Holly said that Dodie threatened her mom, but she didn't figure out what Dodie was saying until her mom started to throw up that morning. That's how she was able to get her mom to the hospital so fast. She told Sharon what she had done and what Dodie had said."

Richard's face had an odd look on it. He seemed to be trying to signal something to Chaz behind Korine's back as she poured herself a cup of coffee. She caught the pointing, though.

Looking down to see what he was gesturing at, she caught the swirl of pink fluff around her ankles as she realized that the nightgown she'd worn was longer by a chiffon ruffle than the terry bathrobe. Blushing, Korine was caught between the desire to laugh at herself for being embarrassed at wearing the negligee, or laughing at the look on Chaz's face as he realized that his mother was wearing such a thing.

"I decided I might as well wear it; I'd always wanted one. Ari said it wasn't evidence, so I got to keep it."

"Ari?" Richard and Chaz said together.

"Detective Sudley to you," she replied with a smile.

She could sense them looking speculatively at each other, then at her retreating back as she returned, humming, to her room to dress for the trip back to Pine Grove. Laughing, she shut the door behind her. Let them wonder.

HARLEQUIN®
INTRIGUE®
WE'LL LEAVE YOU BREATHLESS!

If you've been looking for thrilling tales of contemporary passion and sensuous love stories with taut, edge-of-the-seat suspense—then you'll love Harlequin Intrigue!

Every month, you'll meet six new heroes who are guaranteed to make your spine tingle and your pulse pound. With them you'll enter into the exciting world of Harlequin Intrigue— where your life is on the line and so is your heart!

THAT'S INTRIGUE—
ROMANTIC SUSPENSE
AT ITS BEST!

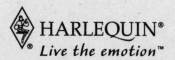

HARLEQUIN®
Live the emotion™